U0025438

Dracula

原著 BRAM STOKER
改寫 DAVID A. HILL
譯者 蘇祥慧

吸血鬼德古拉

About this Book

For the Student

 Listen to the story and do some activities on your Audio CD.

 Talk about the story.

For the Teacher

Go to our Readers Resource site for information on using readers and downloadable Resource Sheets, photocopiable Worksheets, and Tapescripts. www.helblingreaders.com

You can download the Answer Key from the official site of Cosmos Publisher: www.icosmos.com.tw

For lots of great ideas on using Graded Readers consult Reading Matters, the Teacher's Guide to using Helbling Readers.

Structures

Sequencing of future tenses	• Could / was able to / managed to
Present perfect plus yet, already, just	• Had to / didn't have to
First conditional	• Shall / could for offers
Present and past passive	• May / can / could for permission • Might for future possibility
How long?	• Make and let
Very / really / quite	• Causative have • Want / ask / tell someone to do something

Structures from lower levels are also included.

CONTENTS

About the Author

Bram (Abraham) Stoker was born in Dublin, Ireland in 1847. His father was a civil servant[1]. Stoker was ill throughout his childhood, but later excelled[2] at sport when he went to Trinity College, Dublin, where he studied mathematics.

Stoker became a clerk[3] in the Civil Service in 1870, but his great interest was in the theater. He carefully followed the acting career of one of the greatest actors of the time – Sir Henry Irving. In 1878 Irving asked Stoker to become the business manager of the Lyceum Theater in London. In the same year, Stoker married Florence Balcombe. Their only son, Irving Noel, was born the following year.

From early on in his career Stoker published theater reviews[4] and some short stories in newspapers and magazines, and by 1890 he published his first Gothic[5] horror[6] novel, *The Snake's Pass*. In London he became well-known in the literary and artistic[7] world, and was friends with many famous writers.

He also traveled abroad with Irving, and especially enjoyed trips to the USA, where he twice visited The White House and met the President. Real fame came to Stoker in 1897 with the publication of *Dracula*, which soon became very popular.

When Irving died in 1905, Stoker wrote a biography[8] of him. He also suffered a stroke[9], at this time. He recovered and continued writing until he died in 1912.

1 civil servant 公務員
2 excel [ɪkˋsɛl] (v.) 突出
3 clerk [klɝk] (n.) 辦事員
4 review [rɪˋvju] (n.) 評論
5 Gothic [ˋgɑθɪk] (a.) 氣氛詭異之哥德式小說的
6 horror [ˋhɔrɚ] (n.) 恐怖
7 artistic [ɑrˋtɪstɪk] (a.) 藝術的
8 biography [baɪˋɑgrəfɪ] (n.) 傳記
9 stroke [strok] (n.) 中風

About the Book

The story of ***Dracula*** (1897) takes place in Transylvania in Romania, London, Exeter and Whitby in England, and Varna and Galatz on the Black Sea. It is written in what is known as an epistolary[1] style. This means that several characters tell their parts of the story through journal[2] and diary entries[3], letters, telegrams, newspaper articles and a ship's log[4].

In the story the young English solicitor[5], Jonathan Harker visits Count[6] Dracula in his Transylvanian castle to advise him on buying a property[7] in London. Harker has terrible experiences there, and realizes that Dracula and three women in the castle are all vampires[8].

1 epistolary [ɪ`pɪstə,lɛrɪ] (a.) 書信體的
2 journal [`dʒɝnl] (n.) 雜誌；期刊
3 entry [`ɛntrɪ] (n.) 條目
4 ship's log 航海日誌
5 solicitor [sə`lɪsətɚ] (n.) 初級律師
6 count [kaʊnt] (n.) 伯爵
7 property [`prɑpɚtɪ] (n.) 房地產
8 vampire [`væmpaɪr] (n.) 吸血鬼
9 defeat [dɪ`fit] (v.) 戰勝；擊敗
10 theme [θim] (n.) 主題
11 modernity [mɑ`dɝnətɪ] (n.) 現代性
12 cope with 處理；對付
13 invasion [ɪn`veʒən] (n.) 入侵
14 invade [ɪn`ved] (v.) 侵入；侵略
15 destroy [dɪ`strɔɪ] (v.) 毀滅
16 deal with 處理
17 scholar [`skɑlɚ] (n.) 學者

Dracula moves to England and Harker and his young wife Mina become involved in a life-and-death chase to catch and stop him before it is too late.

The story is a classic horror adventure, in which good defeats[9] evil. It also brings up the theme[10] of modernity[11], which was important at that time.

The Victorian age brought about great change and many people believed that society was unable to cope with[12] events. Other people have interpreted *Dracula* as an "invasion[13]" story – Britain is invaded[14] by an evil foreigner who will destroy[15] everyone by turning them all into vampires until someone stops him.

The story also deals with[16] relationships between men and women. Some scholars[17] have suggested that the character of Dracula is based on Prince Vlad III of Wallachia (now Romania). He was known as Dracula, from the word for "dragon".

Before Reading

1 Look at these pictures of some of the main characters from the story. Write some sentences to describe each of them. What do you think each person is like?

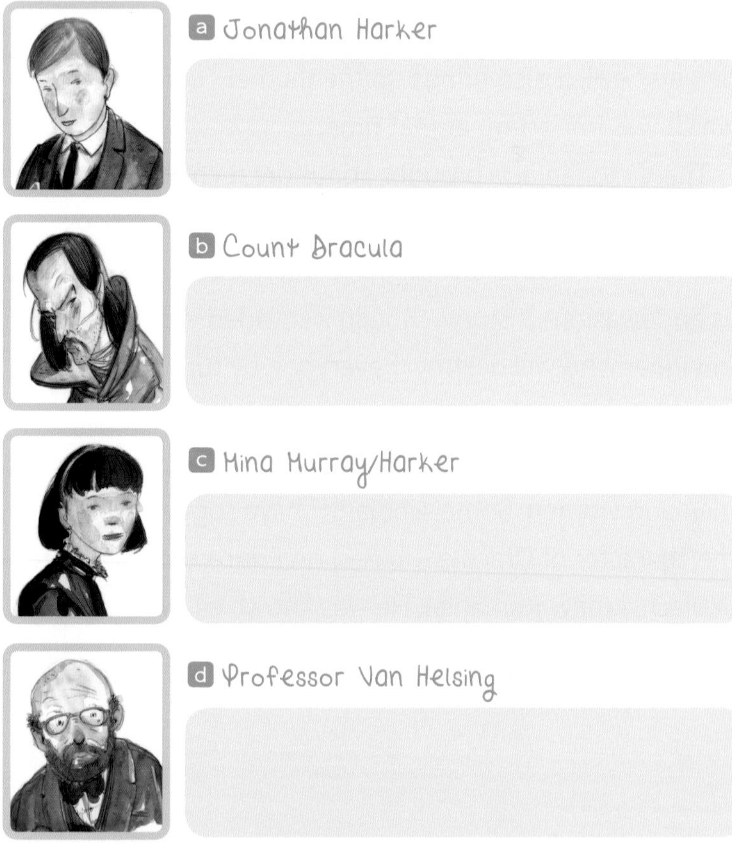

2 Work with one or two other people. Compare your descriptions of the characters.

3 Jonathan Harker is a solicitor. Which of these descriptions explains what a solicitor does?

____ a The person who makes decisions in a court of law, and says what should happen to criminals.

____ b The person who defends a criminal in a court of law.

____ c The person who advises people about law and prepares legal documents about businesses, property, etc.

4 Count Dracula is a vampire. What kind of animals are associated with vampires? Tick. Why?

a a rat ☐

b a wolf ☐

c a bat ☐

d an owl ☐

5 What do you know about vampires? Make some notes, and then share your ideas with a partner.

6 *Dracula* is a horror story. What kinds of things do you expect to find in a horror story? Make lists under these headings. Then compare your notes with a partner.

- (a) characters
- (b) places
- (c) actions
- (d) animals
- (e) weather
- (f) time

7 **Look at the map and read the place names. Can you write the names on the lines?**

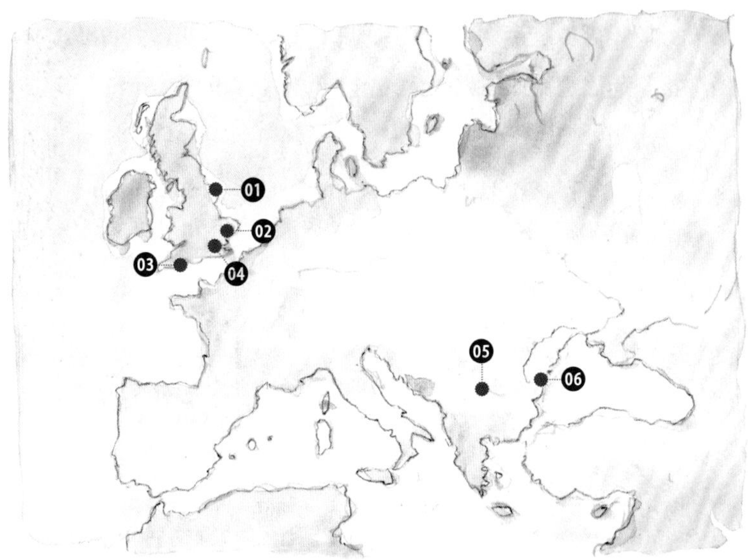

_____ ⓐ Transylvania
_____ ⓑ London
_____ ⓒ Varna
_____ ⓓ Whitby
_____ ⓔ Exeter
_____ ⓕ Purfleet

8 Listen and check. Then match the places with the descriptions.

_____ (a) This is where Count Dracula buys some houses.

_____ (b) This is where Lucy and Mina are on holiday, and where Dracula's ship comes to land.

_____ (c) This is where Count Dracula buys a big house called Carfax, next to a mental hospital.

_____ (d) This is where Jonathan and Mina Harker live, and where Professor Van Helsing visits them.

_____ (e) This is where Count Dracula's castle is.

_____ (f) This is where they wait for Dracula's boat.

9 Match the words from the story to the pictures.

_____ (a) coffin
_____ (b) bench
_____ (c) earth
_____ (d) razor
_____ (e) throat
_____ (f) cart
_____ (g) pin
_____ (h) lizard

1 2 3 4

5 6 7 8

10 Complete the sentences from the story with words from Exercise **9**.

a The ship has a cargo of wooden boxes filled with ______________.

b The Count moved with great speed, like a ______________.

c Later Arthur said goodbye to Lucy, whose body was then put into the ______________.

d My ______________ must have hurt Lucy, for there are two little red marks on her neck.

e We spent today sitting on our ______________.

f I was shaving and I cut my face with the ______________.

g Lucy held her ______________ and looked tired and paler than usual.

h A horse-drawn ______________ carrying lots of large, empty, wooden boxes came into the courtyard.

Chapter 1

3

Where we meet Jonathan Harker, a young solicitor from London, and learn about his journey to Transylvania to the castle of Count Dracula.

Jonathan Harker's Journal

3 May, Bistritz. I have passed through Munich, Vienna and Budapest and am on my way to Transylvania. My impression is that we have left the West and have entered[1] the East. My client, Count Dracula, lives on the borders[2] of three states[3]: Transylvania, Moldavia, and Bukovina, in the center of the Carpathian Mountains. It seems to be one of the wildest and least-known places in Europe. I could not find a map showing exactly where he lives, but I found Bistritz, a town nearby.

As I traveled towards it on the train, I looked out of the window at little towns and castles on steep[4] hills, and at wide rivers and streams[5]. The countryside was beautiful, but strange.

When I arrived at the hotel in Bistritz, there was a letter waiting for me:

1 enter [ˋɛntɚ] (v.) 進入
2 border [ˋbɔrdɚ] (n.) 邊境；國界
3 state [stet] (n.) 國家
4 steep [stip] (a.) 陡峭的
5 stream [strim] (n.) 小河；溪流

4

My friend,

Welcome! I look forward to[1] meeting you.

At three tomorrow you have a place on the coach[2] for Bukovina which travels through the Borgo Pass[3]. My carriage[4] will meet you at the Borgo Pass and bring you here.

Your friend,

Dracula

4 May. As I was leaving the hotel, I asked about Count Dracula but the landlord and his wife made the sign of the cross[5] and refused to speak.

The landlady said: "Must you go? Herr Harker, must you go? It is the eve of St George's Day[6], and after midnight all the evil things in the world will be out."

She then gave me the crucifix[7] from her neck to wear. I felt frightened.

1 look forward to 期待（後接名詞或動名詞）
2 coach [kotʃ] (n.) 四輪大馬車
3 pass [pæs] (n.) 山隘；關口
4 carriage [ˋkærɪdʒ] (n.) 四輪馬車
5 cross [krɔs] (n.) 十字形
6 St George's Day 聖喬治節（4 月 23 日）
7 crucifix [ˋkrusə͵fɪks] (n.) 十字架
8 polyglot [ˋpalɪ͵glat] (a.) 用數種語言書寫的

5 **5 May, the Castle.** From the coach I heard the driver and landlady repeating some words which I didn't understand. I checked them in my polyglot[8] dictionary: "Ordog" – Satan[9], "Pokol" – hell[10], "stregoica" – witch[11], "vrolok" and "vlkoslak" – were wolf or vampire. (I need to ask my client about these things.)

As I was leaving, the people outside the hotel made the sign of the cross and pointed two fingers towards me. One of the other passengers[12] explained that this was to guard me against the evil eye.

9 Satan [ˋsetn̩] (n.) 撒旦；魔鬼
10 hell [hɛl] (n.) 地獄
11 witch [wɪtʃ] (n.) 女巫
12 passenger [ˋpæsn̩dʒɚ] (n.) 乘客

6 We drove fast into the Carpathian Mountains. The driver only stopped once to light the lamps on the coach. At last we saw the Borgo Pass in front of us. There were dark clouds above it and the air was heavy and oppressive[1]. The only light was from our own lamps. The white sandy road stretched[2] in front of us, but there was no carriage waiting for me.

Finally, the driver said: "There is no carriage here. Come to Bukovina with us, Herr Harker. You can return tomorrow."

But, when he finished speaking, our horses began to neigh[3] and snort[4] and, suddenly, four coal-black horses appeared beside our coach. They were driven by a tall man with a long brown beard and a black hat that hid his face. His eyes seemed red in the light of the lamps and he had red lips and sharp-looking teeth that were as white as ivory[5].

He said to the driver, "You are early tonight, my friend."

I got into the carriage and without a word we drove off into the darkness. It was cold and I pulled a cloak[6] around my shoulders and a blanket across my knees. I felt frightened. It was nearly midnight. I heard the howling[7] of wolves from the mountains. The horses shook with fear[8], but the driver was not disturbed at all. It suddenly got much colder, snow fell and soon everything was white. The wolves' howling got nearer.

1 oppressive [ə`prɛsɪv] (a.) 沈重的
2 stretch [strɛtʃ] (v.) 延伸
3 neigh [ne] (v.) (馬)嘶
4 snort [snɔrt] (v.) 噴鼻息
5 ivory [`aɪvərɪ] (n.) 象牙
6 cloak [klok] (n.) 斗篷;披風
7 howl [haʊl] (v.) 怒吼
8 fear [fɪr] (n.) 恐懼

Darkness

- What happens here in the darkness?
- What do you associate with the darkness?
- Are you are afraid of the dark?

Then, I saw a faint[1] blue flame[2] through the darkness. The driver stopped, jumped down and disappeared towards it. The howling got closer and the driver appeared again. We continued but I think we were driving in circles[3]. It was like a nightmare.

The driver got down again and again. The last time, he moved further away than before. Just then the moon came out from behind the clouds and I saw a ring[4] of wolves around us with white teeth and red tongues.

I called out and, suddenly, I saw the driver standing in the roadway, moving his arms as if pushing something away. The wolves moved backwards and disappeared.

We moved quickly through the darkness until we stopped in front of a huge, dark, ruined[5] castle.

1 faint [fent] (a.) 微弱的
2 flame [flem] (n.) 火焰
3 circle [ˋsɝkḷ] (n.) 圓圈
4 ring [rɪŋ] (n.) 圈
5 ruined [ˋruɪnd] (a.) 毀壞的
6 mysterious [mɪsˋtɪrɪəs] (a.) 神祕的
7 knocker [ˋnɑkɚ] (n.) 門環
8 moustache [məsˋtæʃ] (n.) 八字鬍

Chapter 2

Where Jonathan Harker enters the castle of Count Dracula and learns more about his mysterious[6] client.

Jonathan Harker's Journal (continued)

5 May. I stood in front of the huge, dark castle and waited. I began to have all sorts of doubts and fears. What type of terrible adventure was this? Is it normal for a solicitor to be sent to a strange land? To come all this way to explain to a client, a foreigner, how to buy a house in London?

There was no knocker[7] or bell but suddenly the huge main door opened. A tall man, with a long moustache[8] and dressed in black, stood there.

"Welcome to my house!" he said. "Enter freely and of your own will."

As I stepped inside, he shook my hand. It seemed cold like a dead man's hand.

"Count Dracula?" I asked.

"I am Dracula," he replied. "Welcome, Mr Harker. Come and eat and rest."

9 He carried my luggage up a winding[1] stair and along a stone passage[2], and opened a heavy door. I was delighted to see a well-lit room with a table laid for supper and a log fire. There was also a large bedroom with another fire.

"Please sit and eat," said the Count. "Excuse me for not joining you, but I have dined[3] already."

After dinner, we talked by the fire together, and I observed[4] his appearance. He had a thin nose and a high forehead, with lots of hair at the back of his head. His eyebrows were massive[5] and nearly met over his nose. The mouth under his moustache looked rather cruel, with strange, sharp white teeth which showed over his very red lips. He had pointed ears and pale[6] skin. His hands were broad[7] with long fingers and long sharp nails that were cut to a point. Strangely there was hair on his palms[8].

The Count moved towards me and his hands touched me. Suddenly I felt sick.

Eventually he said: "You must be tired. You can sleep as long as you like. I will be away until tomorrow afternoon."

7 May. I slept until late. Breakfast was waiting for me. After eating, I found a library full of English books! I began to look at them. Suddenly, I looked up and saw the Count.

"I am glad you found my library," he said. "These books have given me many hours of pleasure."

1 winding [ˋwaɪndɪŋ] (a.) 彎彎曲曲的
2 passage [ˋpæsɪdʒ] (n.) 通道
3 dine [daɪn] (v.) 進餐；用餐
4 observe [əbˋzɝv] (v.) 注意到；觀察
5 massive [ˋmæsɪv] (a.) 粗大的
6 pale [pel] (a.) 蒼白的
7 broad [brɔd] (a.) 寬闊的
8 palm [pɑm] (n.) 手掌

10 "Can I come to the library when I want?" I asked.

"Certainly," he answered. "You may go anywhere in the castle, except where the doors are locked."

I then asked him about the blue flames from the night before.

He said: "Some people believe that last night was the night when evil spirits[1] rule and that the blue flames burn where treasure is hidden. But most people stay at home because they are frightened, so the treasure remains[2] where it is."

Later, we looked at the papers and documents[3] for his house in London and, since he wanted to buy several properties in England, I told him about another big but old and lonely estate[4] called Carfax, which was beside an asylum[5].

8 May. I thought I was writing too much detail in this diary but now I am glad because writing the facts helps stop my imagination from going wild.

This morning I hung my shaving mirror on the window and I was shaving, when suddenly I felt the Count's hand on my shoulder.

He said: "Good morning".

I jumped, because I couldn't see him in the mirror, and I cut my face with the razor.

I turned to greet the Count, and when I turned back I noticed again that there was no reflection[6] of him in the mirror. I was surprised and I began to feel uneasy.

Then the Count saw the blood on my face, his eyes blazed[7], and he put his hand out to my throat.

I moved back, and his hand touched the landlady's crucifix, and he changed expression[8] immediately.

"Be careful how you cut yourself. It is more dangerous than you think in this country," he said. Then he took my shaving mirror and said: "And this has caused the problem, a terrible tool of man's vanity[9]."

He opened the window and threw the mirror down into the courtyard, where it broke into pieces. Then he left without a word.

I had breakfast alone. I have not seen the Count eat or drink yet. Why is that? After breakfast, I explored[10] the castle and found a room which had a magnificent[11] southern view over forests and river valleys. I realized the castle was on the edge[12] of a terrible precipice[13] – a drop of 300 meters!

I then explored further. There were doors everywhere, but they were all locked. There was no way to get out except through the windows. I am a prisoner[14]!

1 spirit [ˋspɪrɪt] (n.) 靈魂；幽靈
2 remain [rɪˋmen] (v.) 保持
3 document [ˋdɑkjəmənt] (n.) 文件
4 estate [ɪsˋtet] (n.) 地產
5 asylum [əˋsaɪləm] (n.) 精神病院
6 reflection [rɪˋflɛkʃən] (n.) 倒影
7 blaze [blez] (v.) 燃燒；閃耀
8 expression [ɪkˋsprɛʃən] (n.) 表情
9 vanity [ˋvænətɪ] (n.) 虛榮
10 explore [ɪkˋsplor] (v.) 探索
11 magnificent [mægˋnɪfəsənt] (a.) 壯麗的
12 edge [ɛdʒ] (n.) 邊緣
13 precipice [ˋprɛsɪpɪs] (n.) 斷崖
14 prisoner [ˋprɪzṇɚ] (n.) 囚犯

Chapter 3

Where Jonathan Harker realizes he is alone in the castle with the Count and three young "women".

Jonathan Harker's Journal (continued)

I saw the Count making my bed, so there are no servants[1]. This frightens me, because it means that he was driving the carriage the night that I arrived and he controlled the wolves.

12 May. Yesterday evening, the Count asked me about legal[2] matters in England: could he have two solicitors or more, and in different parts of the country?

"Certainly," I replied. "People who do not want one person to know all of their business often have more than one solicitor."

He suddenly asked: "Have you written to your employer[3], Mr Hawkins in Exeter, or anyone else since you arrived?"

"No," I answered, "because I do not see how I can send letters."

"Then write," he said. "Say you will stay here for a month."

"Do you want me to stay for so long?" I asked, my heart growing cold.

"Yes," he answered. "And please only write about business."

I realized he wanted to read the letters before posting[4] them, so I wrote formal notes to Mr Hawkins and to my dear girlfriend, Mina. The Count wrote several notes, then he left the room. I saw they were to someone in Whitby in northeast England, to a German in Varna, Bulgaria, and to a bank in London.

On returning, he said: "I must work this evening. Let me warn you not to fall asleep in other parts of the castle. Hurry back here where you are safe."

Later. I went up to the room with the southern view. I felt like a prisoner. The moonlight was as bright as day. I leaned[5] out of the window and saw the Count coming out of a window one floor lower, and crawling[6] down the castle wall. He moved with great speed, like a lizard[7]. I felt terribly afraid.

15 May. I saw the Count leave in his lizard way again. I explored the castle, and finally entered another room by pushing the door hard.

Moonlight flooded[8] through the windows. I felt comfortable here so I sat at a little desk and wrote this diary.

1 servant [ˋsɝvənt] (n.) 僕人
2 legal [ˋligḷ] (a.) 法律上的
3 employer [ɪmˋplɔɪɚ] (n.) 雇主
4 post [post] (v.) 郵寄
5 lean [lin] (v.) 倚；靠
6 crawl [krɔl] (v.) 爬行
7 lizard [ˋlɪzɚd] (n.) 蜥蜴
8 flood [flʌd] (v.) 淹沒

16 May. Last night I went back to the room. After writing my diary, I felt sleepy. I remembered the Count's warning, but I decided to sleep there. I lay on an old sofa and looked out at the moonlit view.

I suppose I fell asleep, but I fear that what I saw was real. I saw three young women with the moonlight behind them, but they had no shadows. Two were dark, and reminded me of the Count, and the other had wavy, golden hair and blue eyes. Each one had white shiny teeth and red lips. I felt afraid but I wanted to kiss them.

They whispered and laughed in a strange inhuman[1] way. The two dark women said: "Go on! You are first. He is young and strong; there are kisses for all of us."

I lay, looking under my eyelashes[2] as the fair girl bent over me. I felt her breath on me. She licked her lips like an animal; then I felt her two sharp teeth pushing against the skin of my neck.

At that moment, I was conscious[3] of the presence of the Count. In a terrific rage[4] he took hold of the woman. His red eyes blazed in fury[5]. He threw her across the room and made a gesture[6] to the other two. It was the same gesture he used to control the wolves on the night I arrived. His voice was only a whisper, but it rang out[7].

1 inhuman [ɪn`hjumən] (a.) 非人類的
2 eyelash [`aɪ,læʃ] (n.) 睫毛
3 conscious [`kɑnʃəs] (a.) 有意識到的
4 rage [redʒ] (n.) 狂怒
5 fury [`fjʊrɪ] (n.) 狂怒
6 gesture [`dʒɛstʃɚ] (n.) 手勢
7 ring out 發出清晰的聲音

"How dare[1] you touch him when I have forbidden[2] it? He belongs to me. But I promise you that when I have finished with him, you shall kiss him as much as you want. Now go!"

"Are we to have nothing tonight?" asked one of them, pointing to a bag he had thrown on the floor. The bag moved as if there was something alive inside it.

He nodded. One woman jumped forward and opened it. I heard a child crying. Then they disappeared with the terrible bag, fading[3] into the rays[4] of the moonlight and passing out through the window.

Horror overcame[5] me and I became unconscious[6].

Horror

- What two horrific things does Jonathan Harker witness in the scene with the three women?
- Do you like horror films or stories? Tell a horror story to a friend.

1 how dare 竟敢
2 forbid [fɚˋbɪd] (v.) 禁止（動態三態：forbid; forbade, forbad; forbidden）
3 fade [fed] (v.) 逐漸消失
4 ray [re] (n.) 光線
5 overcome [ˌovɚˋkʌm] (v.) 壓倒（動態三態：overcome; overcame; overcome）
6 unconscious [ʌnˋkɑnʃəs] (a.) 不省人事的
7 definitely [ˋdɛfənɪtlɪ] (adv.) 明確地
8 scared [skɛrd] (a.) 嚇壞的
9 cart [kɑrt] (n.) 四輪運貨車
10 gypsy [ˋdʒɪpsɪ] (n.) 吉普賽人

Chapter 4

16

Where Jonathan Harker decides that Count Dracula is definitely[7] not human and that he has many reasons to be scared[8] of him.

Jonathan Harker's Journal (continued)

I awoke in my own bed. I think the Count carried me here.

18 May. I went to look at the room in daylight, but the door was locked, so I fear it wasn't a dream.

17 June. Two large horse-drawn carts[9] carrying lots of large, empty, wooden boxes came into the courtyard with some gypsies[10]. The gypsies unloaded[11] the boxes and left.

24 June. I went to watch for the Count last night again. The gypsies are working somewhere – I can hear the sound of spades[12].

11 unload [ʌnˋlod] (v.) 卸下貨物
12 spade [sped] (n.) 鏟子

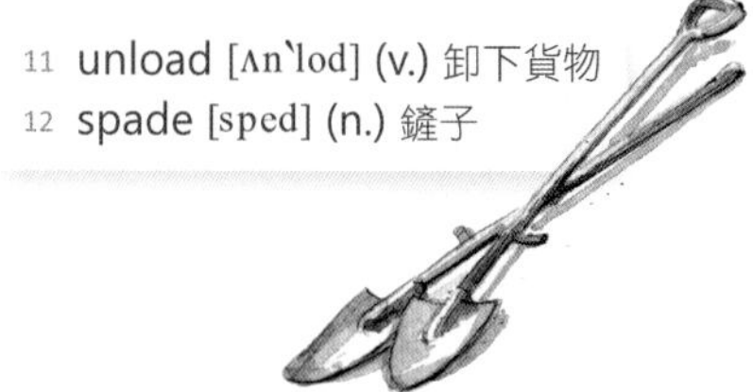

17

Later, I saw him come out of his window. As I waited for his return, I noticed some pretty little specks[1] floating[2] in the moonlight. The specks danced in front of me, almost hypnotizing[3] me, until they changed into the three women from the night before. I ran screaming[4] back to my room.

Suddenly I heard a woman crying in the courtyard. I opened my window and she shouted up at me: "Monster, give me my child!" Then she beat violently[5] at the great door.

I heard the Count calling out and the wolves answered him with their howls. A pack[6] of wolves ran into the courtyard. The woman stopped crying and the wolves left, licking their lips.

How can I escape[7] from this terrible nightmare?

25 June, morning. I realized that I have always been in danger and now I am afraid at night. I have never seen the Count in the daylight, Maybe he sleeps while we are awake. I decided to try and get into his room. I shall try to crawl over to his window. Goodbye, my dearest Mina if I fail.

Same day, later. I got safely back! I took off my boots and climbed across the big rough[8] stones. The Count's room was empty except for dusty furniture, and a heap[9] of golden coins.

There was a door in a corner that led down a dark, circular stairway[10]. At the bottom, I opened another door into a ruined chapel[11] which was used as a graveyard[12].

1 speck [spɛk] (n.) 微小物
2 float [flot] (v.) 漂浮
3 hypnotize [`hɪpnə,taɪz] (v.) 施以催眠術
4 scream [skrim] (v.) 尖叫
5 violently [`vaɪələntlɪ] (adv.) 猛烈地
6 pack [pæk] (n.) 一群
7 escape [ə`skep] (v.) 逃脫
8 rough [rʌf] (a.) 粗糙的

(18) The wooden boxes from yesterday were on the floor. The Count was lying in one of them. He was either dead or asleep. His eyes were stony[13], his cheeks warm and his lips still red, but there was no breath or beating of the heart.

I wanted to search him for his keys, but there was such a look of hate in his dead eyes, that I left and crawled back.

29 June. This morning the Count said: "Tomorrow, my friend, we must part. You return to England, and I am leaving to complete[14] some work, so we may never meet again. The gypsies still have work to do, and the carts will come back. My carriage will take you to the Borgo Pass to meet the coach to Bistritz."

9 heap [hip] (n.) 一堆
10 stairway [ˋstɛr͵we] (n.) 樓梯
11 chapel [ˋtʃæpḷ] (n.) 小禮拜堂
12 graveyard [ˋgrev͵jɑrd] (n.) 墓地
13 stony [ˋstonɪ] (a.) 冷酷的
14 complete [kəmˋplit] (v.) 完成

I was suspicious[1], so I asked: "Why may I not go tonight?"

"Because my coachman[2] and horses are away on business."

"But I could walk."

"Do not stay an hour extra against your will[3], my friend," he said with a soft smile.

I followed him downstairs, but when he opened the main door, the howling of the wolves outside was loud and angry. I knew I could not go against the Count's wishes. With "friends" like these I could do nothing against him.

"Shut the door! I will wait until morning," I shouted.

He slammed[4] the door shut. In silence I went to my room. Count Dracula kissed his hand towards me, with a red light of triumph[5] in his eyes.

Guest or Prisoner?

- Does Jonathan Harker feel like a guest or a prisoner?
- What is stopping Jonathan from leaving?
- Why do you think the Count wants to keep Jonathan in the castle?

30 June, morning. As soon as morning came, I felt safe. I ran down the hall to the front door, but it was locked. I desperately[6] needed to get the key. Without thinking I ran back upstairs and climbed out of my window and over to the Count's room.

I went in, opened the door and went down into the old chapel again. The Count's box was in the same place. The lid was on it, with the nails ready to be hammered[7] down. I knew I needed to search the Count for the key to get out so I lifted the lid and rested it against the wall.

The Count looked much younger. His hair and moustache were dark grey, and his mouth was redder than before.

I couldn't find the keys. The thought that I was helping him to go to London to feed on people's blood for years, drove me mad[8]. I wanted to kill him. I picked up a spade and hit his hateful face.

But as I did so the head turned, and his horrible eyes stared[9] at me. The spade turned in my hand and I hit his forehead. Then the lid fell, hiding him from my sight.

London

- Why does Jonathan think the Count wants to go to London?
- What do you think London was like in Jonathan Harker's time?
- What is London like now?

1 suspicious [sə`spɪʃəs] (a.) 疑心的
2 coachman [`kotʃmən] (n.) 馬車夫
3 will [wɪl] (n.) 意願
4 slam [slæm] (v.) 猛地關上
5 triumph [`traɪəmf] (n.) 勝利
6 desperately [`dɛspərɪtlɪ] (adv.) 絕望地
7 hammer [`hæmɚ] (v.) 錘打
8 drive sb mad 令某人抓狂
9 stare [stɛr] (v.) 凝視

21

I then heard the sound of carts and voices. The gypsies were coming. I ran back up to the Count's room, planning to escape when the door was opened. But nobody entered.

Then I heard a door opening and people moving. When the noise of voices and feet went away, I turned to go back downstairs to the chapel, hoping to find a new entrance[1]. But a sudden wind blew the stair door shut, and I could not open it. I was a prisoner again.

As I write, I can hear the sound of the gypsies moving the boxes and hammering the nails into Dracula's box. I hear voices and moving feet. A door is shut, the key turns; another door opens and shuts, another key turns. I hear the carts and the people in the courtyard, and now they are going off into the distance[2].

I am alone in the castle with these awful[3] women. But I will not remain here. I will climb the castle wall, taking some gold with me. I will find a way out of this terrible place!

1 entrance [ˋɛntrəns] (n.) 入口
2 distance [ˋdɪstəns] (n.) 遠處
3 awful [ˋɔful] (a.) 可怕的

Chapter 5

22 Letter from Miss Mina Murray to Miss Lucy Westenra

9 May.

Dearest Lucy,

Forgive[1] my delay in writing, but the life of a schoolmistress[2] is hard. I am longing[3] to see you, my dear friend, and to be able to talk freely.

I am practicing shorthand[4] for Jonathan. When we are married I will help him with his work. I am also practicing with the typewriter.

We sometimes exchange letters in shorthand, and he is keeping a shorthand journal while he is in Transylvania. I will keep a diary too, when I come to see you.

I have just had a few lines from Jonathan from Transylvania. He is well and he will stay there for about a week. I am longing to hear all of his news. It must be nice to see strange countries. There is the ten o'clock bell ringing. Goodbye.

Your loving,

Mina

Friendship

- Who is Mina writing to?
- Do you ever write to your friends?
- Make a list of all the different ways you can communicate with your friends.

1 forgive [fɚˋgɪv] (v.) 原諒（動詞三態：forgive; forgave; forgiven）
2 schoolmistress [ˋskul,mɪstrɪs] (n.) 女教員
3 long [lɔŋ] (v.) 渴望
4 shorthand [ˋʃɔrt,hænd] (n.) 速記

Chapter 6

23 Mina Murray's Journal

24 July, Whitby. Lucy met me at the station and we drove to The Crescent where she and her mother have rooms.

Whitby is lovely with the immense[1] Abbey[2] ruins and the parish[3] church, both above the town. I am sitting in the churchyard, and I can see the town, the harbor[4] and all the way to the sea.

Lucy told me about Arthur Holmwood, the only son of Lord[5] Godalming, and their coming marriage. That made me sad, as I haven't heard from Jonathan for a month!

26 July. Mr Hawkins sent me a very short letter from Jonathan.

He was very formal but he said that he was on his way home. Something is not right; however, I can feel it.

I am also anxious about Lucy because she has started walking in her sleep again. Her mother and I decided that I should lock the door of our room every night.

3 August. Another week has passed and no news of Jonathan. I hope he is not ill. Each night I am awakened[6] by Lucy moving about the room. She tries the door, and finding it locked, she searches for the key.

6 August. Another three days, and no news. I wish I knew where to write, but nobody has heard from Jonathan since that last letter.

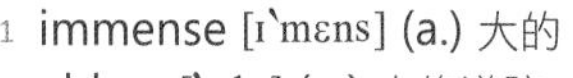

1 immense [ɪˋmɛns] (a.) 大的
2 abbey [ˋæbɪ] (n.) 大修道院
3 parish [ˋpærɪʃ] (n.) 教區
4 harbor [ˋhɑrbɚ] (n.) 港口
5 lord [lɔrd] (n.) 勳爵
6 awaken [əˋwekən] (v.) 清醒

Chapter 7

Taken from "The Dailygraph"

24

8 August, Whitby.

One of the greatest storms on record hit Whitby very suddenly last night. A strange noise was heard around midnight, then the sea roared[1], the wind blew hard and a sea-fog came to the land. There was lightning, and loud thunder that shook everything.

The returning fishing boats were greatly helped by the new searchlight on the cliff[2] top, guiding them into the harbor safely. Suddenly it cleared, and we saw the schooner[3] coming into the harbor. We all shivered[4] when we saw that a dead man was tied to the steering wheel[5]. As the ship crashed[6] into a bank of sand, a huge dog appeared on deck, jumped down and ran straight up the cliff towards the churchyard.

The schooner is called the ***Demeter***. It sailed from Varna, on the Black Sea, to the English coast. It has a cargo[7] of wooden boxes filled with earth. A Whitby solicitor, Mr S.F. Billington, has formally taken possession[8] of the boxes.

The ***Demeter's*** log book[9] was found and it seems some strange and terrible things happened on the ship. First the crew[10] felt the presence of a tall thin man, then one by one the crew disappeared until only the captain was left. He was the dead man found tied to the wheel, with a crucifix in his hand.

1 roar [ror] (v.) 吼叫；呼嘯
2 cliff [klɪf] (n.) 懸崖；峭壁
3 schooner [ˋskunɚ] (n.) 縱帆船
4 shiver [ˋʃɪvɚ] (v.) 發抖；顫抖
5 steering wheel 駕駛盤；方向盤
6 crash [kræʃ] (v.) 撞毀
7 cargo [ˋkɑrgo] (n.) 貨物
8 possession [pəˋzɛʃən] (n.) 擁有
9 log book 航海日誌
10 crew [kru] (n.) 全體船員

Chapter 8

25 Mina Murray's Journal

8 August. Lucy was restless[1] all night. The storm was frightening. She got up and dressed twice, but I put her back to bed.

We went down to the harbor to see the damage from the storm. The sea was still very dark and dangerous.

11 August, 3 a.m. Lucy's bed was empty. I ran outside to find her, and saw her on the opposite cliff, in her nightdress, on our favorite bench[2].

I ran all the way there. At the top I could see something long and black bending over Lucy, with a white face and red, gleaming[3] eyes.

On reaching[4] her, she was alone and she was breathing with difficulty. I put my shawl[5] around her and pinned[6] it at her neck to keep her warm. Then I woke her and helped her home.

Same day, noon. Lucy looks much better. I noticed that, unfortunately, my pin must have hurt her, for there are two little red marks[7] on her neck.

12 August. Twice last night I was disturbed by Lucy trying to get out.

13 August. I woke in the night. Lucy was pointing to a large bat which flew quite close.

14 August. We spent today on our bench. Coming home, we stopped to look at the sunset. Suddenly Lucy murmured[8]: "His red eyes! They are just the same." She was looking towards our seat, where a dark figure[9], with large burning eyes, was sitting.

Lucy went to bed early. I walked outside, thinking of Jonathan. Returning, I saw Lucy leaning out of our window. Sitting beside her was something that looked like a large bird.

I ran to our bedroom, but Lucy was moving back to bed, fast asleep[10]. She held her throat and looked tired and paler than usual.

17 August. Lucy's mother told me that her heart is weak and she may die soon. Lucy does not know this. There is no news from Jonathan, and Lucy seems to be growing weaker.

I keep the key to our room tied on my wrist. At night she walks around and sits at the open window. I looked at my pinpricks[11] on her throat, and saw that the wounds[12] are larger.

1 restless [ˋrɛstlɪs] (a.) 焦躁不安的
2 bench [bɛntʃ] (n.) 長椅
3 gleam [glim] (v.) 閃爍
4 reach [ritʃ] (v.) 到達
5 shawl [ʃɔl] (n.) 方形披巾
6 pin [pɪn] (v.) 用別針釘住
7 mark [mɑrk] (n.) 痕跡
8 murmur [ˋmɝmɚ] (v.) 低聲說
9 figure [ˋfɪgjɚ] (n.) 人形
10 fast asleep 睡得很沉
11 pinprick [ˋpɪn͵prɪk] (n.) 針刺；針孔
12 wound [waund] (n.) 傷口

Diary

- What different things does Mina include in her journal (diary)?
- Why do you think she writes her journal?
- Why is her journal useful for her and for us?
- Do you write a diary?
- What do you write in your diary?
- Do you ever re-read or allow anyone else to read your diary?

27 **Letter from Samuel F. Billington & Son, Solicitors, Whitby to Messrs. Carter, Paterson & Co., London**

17 August.

Dear Sirs,

Enclosed[1] is the invoice[2] for goods sent by Great Northern Railway to King's Cross Station, to be delivered[3] immediately to Carfax, near Purfleet, on arrival tomorrow. Please find enclosed the house keys. Place the fifty boxes in the chapel, marked "A" on the enclosed plan. Please leave the keys in the main hall when you depart[4].

Faithfully yours,

Samuel F. Billington & Son

Boxes

- Whose boxes are mentioned in the letter?
- Where have they come from? Where are they going?
- Why do you think the boxes are important?

28 Mina Murray's Journal

18 August. Lucy is much better. I asked her about that night on the bench.

She said: "I didn't quite dream, and it all seemed real. I wanted to be at the bench, but didn't know why. I was afraid. I vaguely[5] remember something dark with red eyes, like what we saw at sunset, and something very sweet and bitter around me."

1 enclose [ɪn`kloz] (v.)（隨函）附寄
2 invoice [`ɪnvɔɪs] (n.) 發票
3 deliver [dɪ`lɪvɚ] (v.) 投遞
4 depart [dɪ`pɑrt] (v.) 出發；離開
5 vaguely [`veglɪ] (adv.) 模糊地

29 **19 August.** Joy, joy, joy! At last, news of Jonathan. The dear man has been ill. Mr Hawkins sent on a letter. I am leaving this morning to help nurse[1] Jonathan, and bring him home.

Letter from Sister Agatha, Hospital of St Joseph and St Mary, Budapest, to Miss Wilhelmina Murray

12 August.

Dear Madam,

I am writing at the request of Jonathan Harker, who is not strong enough to write. He has been here for six weeks, suffering from a violent brain fever[2]. He sends his love. He needs more rest. Please bring money to pay for his stay.

Yours, with sympathy[3] and blessings[4],

Sister Agatha

P.S. My patient[5] is asleep. I opened the letter to write some more. He has had a terrible shock, and in his delirium[6] talked of wolves, blood, ghosts and demons[7]. I wanted to write before, but we knew nothing about him. He is getting better, and in a few weeks I'm sure he will be well again.

1 nurse [nɝs] (v.) 悉心照料
2 brain fever 腦膜炎
3 sympathy [ˋsɪmpəθɪ] (n.) 同情
4 blessing [ˋblɛsɪŋ] (n.) 祝福
5 patient [ˋpeʃənt] (n.) 病患
6 delirium [dɪˋlɪrɪəm] (n.) 譫妄；（暫時性的）精神錯亂
7 demon [ˋdimən] (n.) 惡魔

Chapter 9

30

Letter from Mina Harker to Lucy Westenra

24 August, Budapest.

Dearest Lucy,

I am here in Budapest. Jonathan is very pale and weak. He has had a terrible shock and doesn't remember anything. However, he gave me his journal to keep. His secret is inside. He says I can read it if I want, but I mustn't tell him what is in there without a serious reason. It is now safely put away.

Lucy, we were married today in the hospital, so Jonathan is now my husband.

Your ever-loving,

Mina Harker

31 Lucy Westenra's Diary

24 August, Hillingham. I must imitate Mina and write things down. Last night I dreamt again. Perhaps it is because I am back home at Hillingham. I am frightened, weak and exhausted[1].

25 August. Another bad night. At midnight I woke up and there was scratching[2] at the window. More bad dreams. I am horribly weak. My face is very pale and my throat hurts me. Mother is not well either.

Letter from Arthur Holmwood to his friend Dr Seward

31 August, Albemarle Hotel.

Dear John,

I need help. Lucy is ill. She looks awful and she is getting worse every day. She has agreed to see you. Go to Hillingham for lunch tomorrow and examine[3] her. I am filled with anxiety[4] and want to talk to you alone as soon as you have seen her.

Arthur

1 exhausted [ɪg`zɔstɪd] (a.) 精疲力竭的
2 scratch [skrætʃ] (v.) 搔；抓
3 examine [ɪg`zæmɪn] (v.) 檢查；診察
4 anxiety [æŋ`zaɪətɪ] (n.) 焦慮

32 Letter from Dr Seward to Arthur Holmwood

2 September, Purfleet Asylum.

My dear friend,

I was sorry you had to visit your father when I was at Hillingham. I hope he is better. I can find no physical[1] reason for Lucy's problems. She seems bloodless[2], but without the usual signs[3] of anaemic[4] patients. It must be something mental[5]. She complains of difficulty in breathing, heavy sleep and dreams which frighten her, but which she cannot remember.

I have asked my old friend and university professor, Professor Van Helsing, to come from Amsterdam. He knows much about such obscure[6] diseases[7].

Yours always,

John Seward

1 physical [ˋfɪzɪkḷ] (a.) 身體的
2 bloodless [ˋblʌdləs] (a.) 貧血的
3 sign [saɪn] (n.) 病症
4 anaemic [əˋnimɪk] (a.) 貧血的
5 mental [ˋmɛntḷ] (a.) 心理的
6 obscure [əbˋskjʊr] (a.) 難理解的
7 disease [dɪˋziz] (n.) 疾病
8 anaemia [əˋnimɪə] (n.) 貧血

Letter from Dr Seward to Arthur Holmwood

3 September, Purfleet Asylum.

My dear Arthur,

Van Helsing came and made a careful examination, and he said that there is no physical cause for her illness. There is blood loss, but no anaemia[8]. But there is always a cause for everything. He has gone home to think. We must send him a telegram every day, and if necessary, he will return.

Yours always,

John Seward

Telegram from Dr Seward, Purfleet, London, to Van Helsing, Amsterdam

6 September. Terrible change for the worse. Come immediately.

Lucy

- What is wrong with Lucy? Who is trying to help her?
- Do they understand what is wrong with Lucy?
- Do you think that Van Helsing will be able to help her?

Chapter 10

34 Dr Seward's Diary

7 September. At Hillingham, Van Helsing saw Lucy and said: "She will die from lack of blood! She must have a transfusion[1] at once[2]."

Arthur was there and agreed to give his blood. Soon life came back into Lucy's cheeks, while Arthur's grew paler and weaker.

Afterwards, as Van Helsing moved the pillow, the black velvet[3] band round Lucy's throat moved, and I saw two holes over the jugular[4] vein[5]. They were not large, but they were unpleasant-looking.

"I must return to Amsterdam tonight," Van Helsing said. "There are books and things I need. Do not let her out of your sight. You must not sleep all night. I shall be back as soon as possible."

9 September. I sat up with Lucy for two nights. I was very tired when I got to Hillingham tonight. Lucy made me a bed on a sofa in the next room, and left the doors open. I slept immediately.

1 transfusion [træns`fjuʒən] (n.) 輸血
2 at once 立刻
3 velvet [`vɛlvɪt] (a.) 天鵝絨的
4 jugular [`dʒʌgjələ] (a.) 頸靜脈的
5 vein [ven] (n.) 靜脈；血管

35 **10 September.** I woke with the Professor's hand on my shoulder.

"How is our patient?" he asked.

"She was well, when she left me," I answered.

But when we entered the bedroom, Lucy was whiter than ever.

"We must begin again," he said. "You must give your blood."

We started the transfusion immediately. When some slight[1] color came back into her cheeks and lips, we stopped.

"Go home and make yourself strong," said the Professor. "I will stay with Lucy tonight. We must watch her, and not let others know. I have serious reasons for this."

11 September. A parcel[2] of garlic[3] flowers arrived for the Professor. In Lucy's room he shut the windows securely, then rubbed[4] the flowers over the frames[5]. He did the same around the door. He then made a wreath[6] of garlic flowers for Lucy's neck.

When Lucy went to bed, he fixed the wreath in place and said: "Take care not to disturb it, and do not open the windows or the door."

Lucy promised him, and then we left.

1 slight [slaɪt] (a.) 輕微的
2 parcel [ˋpɑrsḷ] (n.) 小包
3 garlic [ˋgɑrlɪk] (n.) 大蒜
4 rub [rʌb] (v.) 摩擦
5 frame [frem] (n.) 窗框
6 wreath [riθ] (n.) 花圈

Chapter 11

Dr Seward's Diary

13 September. At Hillingham, Van Helsing and I were met by Mrs Westenra, who said: "I was worried about Lucy last night, so I took the strong-smelling flowers away and opened the window for a bit of fresh air."

The Professor's face turned grey. "As I expected," he murmured as we entered the room. "Today you must operate and I shall provide the blood for the transfusion."

Later he told Mrs Westenra that the flowers were part of the cure[7] and must not be removed[8]. He wanted to watch Lucy tonight.

Lucy Westenra's Diary

17 September. I am getting strong again. My bad dreams have gone. The flapping[9] at the window and the voices that commanded[10] me to do things that I can't remember have stopped, too.

7 cure [kjʊr] (n.) 療法
8 remove [rɪˋmuv] (v.) 移除
9 flap [flæp] (v.) 拍打
10 command [kəˋmænd] (v.) 命令

37 **Night.** Tonight I went to bed, taking care that the flowers were in position[1]. I was wakened by a big bat knocking its wings against the window. Mother came in. I asked her to come in and sleep with me. There was more flapping at the window, followed by a loud crash, and a strong wind blew in. I could see the head of a great grey wolf at the window. Mother cried out in fright, sat up, and tore[2] the flowers from my neck, then fell over dead. A lot of little specks blew in through the broken window, circling around. I tried to move, but could not.

Alone with the dead! I dare not go out. The air seems full of specks, floating and circling in the wind from the window.

1 position [pə`zɪʃən] (n.) 位置
2 tear [tɛr] (v.) 扯掉（動詞三態：tear; tore; torn）
3 rush [rʌʃ] (v.) 衝；匆忙
4 brandy [`brændɪ] (n.) 白蘭地酒
5 gums [gʌmz] (n.)〔複〕齒齦

Chapter 12

Dr Seward's Diary

18 September. A telegram from Van Helsing telling me to watch Lucy last night, arrived twenty-two hours late! I rushed[3] to Hillingham by ten o'clock, but nobody answered the door. Van Helsing arrived and I explained the situation.

"I fear we are too late," he said.

We entered through the kitchen window. In Lucy's bedroom, she and her mother were on the bed. Lucy was white, a look of terror on her face. Her throat showed the two little wounds. Van Helsing listened to Lucy's chest, got some brandy[4] and rubbed it onto Lucy's lips, gums[5], wrists and palms.

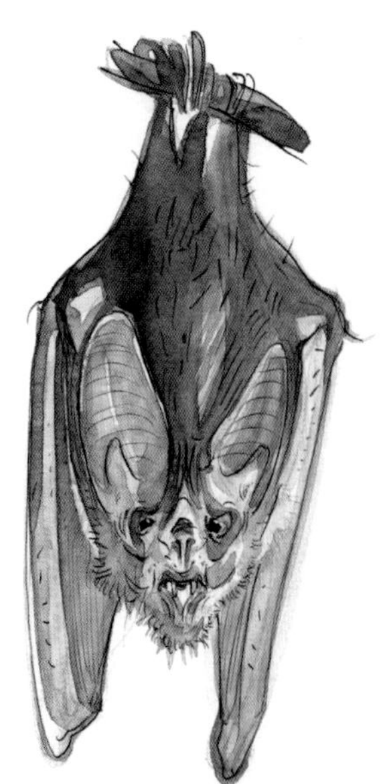

A friend of Arthur's, Quincey Morris, arrived. Arthur, who was looking after his sick father, sent him to find out how Lucy was. He immediately agreed to a transfusion to save Lucy.

39 Afterwards, I found Van Helsing reading Lucy's diary. He gave it to me.

"What does it all mean?" I asked.

"You will understand later," he answered.

19 September. Lucy seemed weaker each time she woke. We noticed that her teeth were growing longer and sharper. In the afternoon we telegraphed Arthur. She brightened a little when he arrived.

20 September. I watched Lucy last night. There was garlic around the windows and doors, and she had the wreath around her neck. Once I saw a large bat circling and hitting the window with its wings. At six o'clock Van Helsing relieved[1] me and bent down to examine Lucy. When he lifted the flowers, the wounds on her neck had gone.

"She is dying," he said. "Wake Arthur!"

Arthur came and sat by her bed, holding her hand.

She said in a soft, voluptuous[2] voice: "Arthur, my love, kiss me!"

Van Helsing immediately jumped up and threw him across the room. "Not for your life!" he said. "Not for your living soul and hers!"

A look of rage crossed Lucy's face, and her sharp teeth showed.

Then her eyes closed and her breathing became difficult and then stopped.

"She is dead," said Van Helsing.

I took Arthur into the sitting-room, where he sat down and sobbed[3], then I returned to Lucy's room.

"There is peace for her at last," I said. "It is the end."

"No," said Van Helsing. "I'm afraid it is only the beginning."

When I asked him what he meant, he shook his head and answered: "Wait and see."

The Kiss

- Why won't Van Helsing allow Lucy to kiss Arthur?
- What kind of kiss does she want to give him? If she kisses him what will happen?
- Do you believe that kisses can be fatal?

1 relieve [rɪˋliv] (v.) 緩和；使放心
2 voluptuous [vəˋlʌptʃuəs] (a.) 縱欲的
3 sob [sɑb] (v.) 嗚咽；啜泣

Chapter 13

41 Dr Seward's Diary

We prepared for Lucy's funeral[1] the next day. Van Helsing looked in her room and found a number of her letters and her diary. He kept them.

Before going to bed, Van Helsing and I went into Lucy's room. Lucy was lying with the sheet[2] over her face, surrounded by white flowers and candles. Van Helsing gently turned back the sheet and we were both amazed[3] at the beauty of Lucy. Van Helsing got some garlic flowers and spread[4] them around Lucy's body, and put a little gold crucifix on her mouth.

"Tomorrow," he said, "I want to cut off her head and take out her heart. I cannot do it tonight, because Arthur will want to see her. When she is in her coffin[5] later, we will do the operation[6] so that nobody knows."

"But why do it at all?" I asked.

"John," he replied, "trust me. There are unpleasant things you don't know about, and strange and terrible days ahead of us."

I took Van Helsing's hand and promised that I trusted him.

1 funeral [ˋfjunərəl] (n.) 葬禮
2 sheet [ʃit] (n.) 床單
3 amazed [əˋmezd] (a.) 吃驚的
4 spread [sprɛd] (v.) 散布（動詞三態：spread; spread; spread）
5 coffin [ˋkɔfɪn] (n.) 棺材；靈柩
6 operation [ˏɑpəˋreʃən] (n.) 操作；手術

42 Van Helsing came into my room early in the morning.

"Do not bother about the operation," he said. "It is too late. The little crucifix was stolen by one of the servants. Now we must wait."

Later Arthur arrived to say goodbye to Lucy, whose body was then put into the coffin.

Van Helsing kept watch over Lucy's coffin all night.

Mina Harker's Journal

22 September, train to Exeter. Today we were in central London and walked down Piccadilly. Jonathan was holding me by the arm.

I was looking at a beautiful girl sitting in a carriage when I felt Jonathan clutch[1] my arm tightly. I turned to him quickly and I saw that he was very pale. He was staring in terror at a tall, thin man with a long nose and a black moustache and beard.

The man was also looking at the girl and he didn't notice us. I looked at him carefully. He had a hard, cruel face with big white teeth and very red lips.

The Man

- Who is the man? Share ideas with a partner.

1 clutch [klʌtʃ] (v.) 抓住

43

"Do you see who it is?" Jonathan asked.

"No, dear," I said. "I don't know him. Who is it?"

"It is the Count!" he answered. "But he has grown younger."

Jonathan was very distressed[1]. The man moved away, and we went and sat in Green Park.

It was a hot day and we found a comfortable seat in a shady[2] place. After a few minutes Jonathan's eyes closed and he fell asleep[3], with his head on my shoulder.

When he awoke, he had forgotten about the stranger, and we caught the train back to Exeter.

In the evening a telegram from Van Helsing told us that Mrs Westenra and Lucy were both dead.

Dr Seward's Diary

22 September. Lucy is buried[4] in Hampstead, close to Hillingham. Arthur has gone back home with his friend, Quincey Morris. Van Helsing is going back to Amsterdam, but he will return tomorrow. He says that he has got work to do in London. He can stay with me when he returns.

1 distressed [dɪˋstrɛst] (a.) 痛苦的
2 shady [ˋʃedɪ] (a.) 陰涼的
3 fall asleep 睡著
4 bury [ˋbɛrɪ] (v.) 埋葬
5 occasion [əˋkeʒən] (n.) 場合

The *Westminster Gazette*, 25 September

A HAMPSTEAD MYSTERY

Recently several young children have come home late after playing on Hampstead Heath. The children say that a mysterious "beautiful lady" asked them to go for a walk with her. This has always happened in the evening and on some occasions[5] the children were only found in the early morning. The children all have wounds in their throats, perhaps made by a rat or small dog. The police are watching carefully any young children in and around the Heath.

The Lady

- Who do you think this lady is?
- Why do you think the children have wounds in their throats?
- Why do you think the lady chose children?
- Do you think this piece of news is scary?

Chapter 14

45 Mina Harker's Journal

24 September. When I came home to Exeter I read Jonathan's journal. What horror! Is it true or only imagination? In Piccadilly he seemed certain about the dark man, and he wrote in his journal that the terrible Count was coming to London. I began writing out his journal with my typewriter.

Letter from Van Helsing to Mrs Harker

24 September.

Dear Madam,

Arthur allowed me to read Lucy's papers. As you were close friends, could I visit you to discuss certain matters?

Van Helsing

Telegram from Mrs Harker to Van Helsing

25 September. Come today at any time you want. Mina Harker

1 recover [rɪˋkʌvɚ] (v.) 恢復
2 arrange [əˋrendʒ] (v.) 安排

 Mina Harker's Journal

25 September. Before Van Helsing arrived I sat at the typewriter and copied out my journal. If he asked about Lucy I could give it to him to read.

When he read it he said: "Madam Mina, this opens a door to me!" Then he asked about Jonathan.

"He had almost recovered[1]," I said. "But in London someone reminded him of the terrible things that led to his brain fever."

"I shall stay in Exeter tonight," he said. "I want to think about everything. Now tell me about your husband's troubles."

Later, I gave him the typewritten version of Jonathan's journal. We arranged[2] to meet in the morning.

Letter from Van Helsing to Mrs Harker

25 September, 6 o'clock.

Dear Madam Mina,

As soon as I got to my hotel I read your husband's journal. You may sleep without doubt. Strange and terrible as it is, it is true! I will have much to ask him when I see him tomorrow morning.

Yours faithfully,

Abraham Van Helsing

Jonathan Harker's Journal

26 September. I know about Van Helsing's visit and that he believes my story about the Count. Now I know that, I am not afraid, not even of the Count! He is in London; it was him I saw. And Van Helsing will hunt him out.

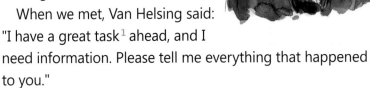

When we met, Van Helsing said: "I have a great task[1] ahead, and I need information. Please tell me everything that happened to you."

This morning, I took him to the station, and got him the papers. He suddenly noticed something in the *Westminster Gazette* and grew white.

He read intently[2], and said to himself: "My God! So soon!"

Van Helsing

- What is Van Helsing's task?
- What did he read in the *Westminster Gazette*?

1 task [tæsk] (n.) 任務
2 intently [ɪn`tɛntlɪ] (adv.) 專注地
3 nod [nɑd] (v.) 點（頭）

48 Dr Seward's Diary

26 September. Van Helsing returned to London this morning.

"What do you think of that?" he asked, giving me the *Westminster Gazette*.

I read about children being taken away and then found with small wounds in their throats.

"It's like poor Lucy's," I said.

"Do you still not understand what Lucy died of? How was all that blood lost?" he asked.

I shook my head, and he went on. "Were the holes in the children's throats made by the same thing that made them in Miss Lucy's throat?"

I nodded[3] my head.

"You are wrong. I wish that was true, but it is far worse. They were made by Miss Lucy!"

Chapter 15

49 Dr Seward's Diary (continued)

"Are you mad?" I shouted.

"I wish I was," he answered. "It is difficult to believe, but tonight I will prove[1] it."

Later that night, we walked to Hampstead churchyard. When we got to the Westenra tomb, Van Helsing opened the lid of Lucy's coffin. It was empty!

Then we went outside to watch for Lucy. It was a long, cold wait, but suddenly I saw something white moving. The Professor went hurriedly towards it. I followed. A dim[2], white figure moved in the direction of the Westenra tomb. Reaching the Professor, I found he was holding a tiny[3] child in his arms.

"Are you satisfied now?" he said.

I lit a match[4] and looked at the child's throat. There was no mark of any kind.

"We were just in time," said the Professor thankfully.

1 prove [pruv] (v.) 證明
2 dim [dɪm] (a.) 微暗的
3 tiny [ˋtaɪnɪ] (a.) 微小的
4 match [mætʃ] (n.) 火柴

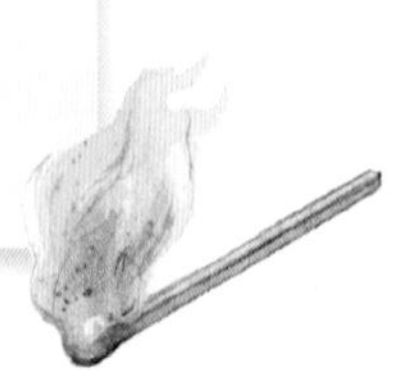

(50) **27 September.** At two o'clock this afternoon, Van Helsing opened the coffin again; there lay Lucy. She was beautiful – her mouth redder, and her cheeks pink.

He pulled back her lips. "See," he said, "her teeth are sharper now, because of these children. Are you convinced[1] now, John? She has been dead a week. Most corpses[2] do not look like this. She is Undead. I will cut off her head, fill her mouth with garlic and drive[3] a stake[4] through her body."

Van Helsing did not perform this dreadful[5] task straight away because he wanted Arthur to understand everything first. He didn't want him to think badly about our actions later.

We arranged to meet together with Arthur and Quincey Morris the next night at his hotel.

Note left by Van Helsing at the Berkeley Hotel, for Dr John Seward

27 September.

Dear John,

I am going back to the churchyard. I don't want the Undead, Miss Lucy, to leave tonight. I shall fix[6] garlic and a crucifix on the door of the tomb to prevent[7] her from going out. But the "other one" has the power to find her tomb. He is cunning[8]. He already fooled[9] us when he played us for Miss Lucy's life and we lost. So, if he goes there tonight, he will find me. I am writing this in case anything happens.

Read the papers that are with this letter, Harker's diary and the rest, then we will find this great Undead, and cut off his head and burn or drive a stake through his heart, so that the world may rest from him.

Van Helsing

Undead

- Who is the "other one" Van Helsing talks about? How is he described?
- What do they plan to do to this great Undead? Why?

1 convinced [kən`vɪnst] (a.) 確信的
2 corpse [kɔrps] (n.) 屍體
3 drive [draɪv] (v.) 把（釘、樁等）打入（動詞三態：drive; drove; driven）
4 stake [stek] (n.) 樁
5 dreadful [`drɛdfəl] (a.) 可怕的
6 fix [fɪks] (v.) 使固定
7 prevent [prɪ`vɛnt] (v.) 防止
8 cunning [`kʌnɪŋ] (a.) 狡猾的
9 fool [ful] (v.) 耍弄

Chapter 16

51 Dr Seward's Diary (continued)

29 September. Last night, Arthur, Quincey and I met Van Helsing in his room at the Berkeley Hotel. We discussed plans. Arthur was against his plans. So we decided to go to Lucy's grave.

At midnight Van Helsing lit a lamp and we stood around Lucy's coffin.

"John," he asked, "was Miss Lucy's body in this coffin yesterday?"

"It was," I replied.

We opened the coffin. It was empty.

He then put some Holy Communion wafers[1] around the tomb.

"So the Undead cannot enter," he explained.

We all went outside and hid. Later, the Professor pointed to a white figure. In the moonlight we saw a fair-haired[2] woman, her face bent over a fair-haired child. The child gave a sharp cry. As she moved towards us we could see that Lucy's sweetness was now cruelty, and her purity was voluptuousness[3].

Van Helsing moved out and gestured to us to join him. We stood in a line in front of the tomb door. He raised his lantern, and we saw the fresh blood trickling[4] from her mouth. We shuddered[5] with horror.

She advanced[6], her eyes blazing, and threw down the child, who lay moaning[7]. She moved towards Arthur with her arms open, saying: "Come to me, Arthur. My arms are hungry for you. Come, my love and we can rest together!"

Her voice had a terrible sweetness to it, and Arthur opened his arms as if in a trance[8], but Van Helsing jumped between them holding up a golden crucifix.

She moved backwards, and with rage in her face, rushed past.

Then Van Helsing said: "Arthur, shall I continue my work?"

"Certainly. There can be no horror like this any more."

Van Helsing removed the holy wafers and Lucy passed back into the coffin. He then put the holy wafers back in place.

"We can do no more until tomorrow," he said. "Be here at two."

29 September. Today, when we opened the coffin, there lay Lucy.

"Is it really Lucy's body?" asked Arthur.

"It is and yet it isn't. But soon you will see her as she was, and is," replied Van Helsing.

1 wafer [ˋwefɚ] (n.) 聖餅
2 fair-haired [ˋfɛrˋhɛrd] (a.) 金髮的
3 voluptuousness [vəˋlʌptʃuəsnɪs] (n.) 肉感；放縱
4 trickle [ˋtrɪkḷ] (v.) 細細地流
5 shudder [ˋʃʌdɚ] (v.) 發抖；戰慄
6 advance [ədˋvæns] (v.) 向前進
7 moan [mon] (v.) 呻吟
8 trance [træns] (n.) 恍神

53 He took his equipment[1] from his bag, including a one-meter, round, wooden stake with a pointed end, and said: "Before we start, let me tell you this. When people become Undead, they cannot die. They continue forever, adding new victims[2], because everyone who dies from the bite of the Undead becomes Undead themselves. This unhappy lady's career[3] has only just begun. Those children whose blood she sucks are not yet in danger, but if she continues, they will change, too. However, if she dies, they will become normal again. When this Undead is changed into a true dead person, then Lucy's soul will be free. So the hand that strikes the blow to set her free is also a blessed hand."

We all looked at Arthur. He stepped forward and said: "Tell me what to do and I will do it."

Van Helsing gave Arthur the stake and a hammer and told him to hammer it through her heart.

As he did so, Van Helsing read out a special prayer for the dead.

The *thing* in the coffin screamed, shook and twisted[4], and blood poured from the heart, but Arthur didn't stop until the body lay still.

When we looked in the coffin, we saw the Lucy we knew, with her sweet, pure face.

1 equipment [ɪˋkwɪpmənt] (n.) 裝備
2 victim [ˋvɪktɪm] (n.) 受害者
3 career [kəˋrɪr] (n.) 生涯
4 twist [twɪst] (v.) 扭曲

54 Arthur turned to Van Helsing and said: "Thank you! You have given my dear Lucy her soul again, and given me peace."

We sent Arthur and Quincey out of the tomb and then cut off the top of the stake, leaving the point in the body. Then we cut off the head and filled the mouth with garlic. We closed up the coffin, gathered our belongings[1] and came out. The Professor locked the door and gave Arthur the key.

"Now, my friends, one step of our work is done. But there remains a greater task: to find the creator of all this sorrow and destroy him. It will be long and difficult, and there will be danger and pain. Will you help me?"

We each took his hand in turn and promised to help.

"In two nights we will meet and dine together," explained the Professor. "Two other people who you do not know will come, and I will tell you my plans."

Step Two

- What step of their work have they completed?
  What is step two of their work?
- Do you think step two will be more difficult than step one?
- Do you know who the two other people are? Try and guess.

Chapter 17

55 Dr Seward's Diary (continued)

When we arrived at the hotel, Van Helsing found a telegram waiting for him.

"Am coming by train. Jonathan is at Whitby.
Important news. Mina"

I collected Mrs Harker and took her home with me. During the evening, I read her husband's journal again, and she copied my diaries with her typewriter.

30 September. Mr Harker and his wife spent the day putting all the journals, letters and other documents into chronological[2] order, to have a clear picture of events. It is strange to think that Carfax, next door to this lunatic[3] asylum where I live, is perhaps the Count's hiding place!

1 belongings [bəˋlɔŋɪŋz] (n.)〔複〕所攜帶之物
2 chronological [ˏkrɑnəˋlɑdʒɪkḷ] (a.) 按時間次序的
3 lunatic [ˋlunəˏtɪk] (a.) 瘋的

Jonathan Harker's Journal

29 September. Met Mr Billington in Whitby to trace[1] the Count's cargo. I saw the invoice for "Fifty cases of common earth", and the Count's letters and instructions. I also got copies of the letters to and from Carter Paterson in London.

30 September. I met the station master at King's Cross and saw the records: the number of boxes was the same. I then went to Carter Paterson's office and saw their documents. I now know that *all* the fifty boxes which arrived in Whitby from Varna on the *Demeter* were put into the chapel at Carfax.

1 trace [tres] (v.) 追蹤
2 limitation [ˌlɪməˋteʃən] (n.) 限制
3 extent [ɪkˋstɛnt] (n.) 程度
4 creature [ˋkritʃɚ] (n.) 動物
5 vanish [ˋvænɪʃ] (v.) 消失
6 reappear [ˌriəˋpɪr] (v.) 再出現

Chapter 18

57

Dr Seward's Diary

30 September. Arthur and Quincey arrived and studied our documents. Later I collected Van Helsing and gave him a copy of everything to read after dinner.

Mina Harker's Journal

30 September. We met in Dr Seward's study. The Professor said: "We have all read the facts. There are such beings as vampires. The vampire which is amongst us is strong and cunning. He can, within limitations[2], appear when and where he wants, and in various forms. He can to some extent[3] control storms, fog and thunder, and creatures[4] such as rats, bats, owls, and wolves. He can change size, vanish[5] and reappear[6]. It is a terrible task we are beginning. Are you all with me in this?"

We stood up, and making a circle of hands, agreed.

Van Helsing continued: "Vampires need the blood of the living, which makes them grow younger. They do not eat, make shadows or reflections, and they are extremely strong.

Our vampire can change himself into a wolf or a bat. He can come in a mist that he creates, and as dust on rays of moonlight. He can enter and leave any place. However, he has limitations. He may not enter any place until he is invited. His power stops with daylight and he must sleep in the boxes of earth he brought from his castle. Some things remove his power: garlic, the crucifix or a rose branch[1] on the coffin all stop him from leaving it. And the stake and the head cut off give him rest, as we have seen with Lucy. Thus, when we find where he lives, we must keep him in his coffin and kill him. Now, we will go next door to see whether the fifty boxes are still there; if not, we must find each one. And finally, Madam Mina, your work is ended now. You are too precious to put at risk."

1 branch [bræntʃ] (n.) 樹枝

Chapter 19

59 Jonathan Harker's Journal

1 October, 5 a.m. We were given a crucifix, a wreath of garlic flowers, a revolver[1], a knife, an electric lamp, and an envelope containing holy wafers.

Seward opened Carfax door with a skeleton key[2].

Van Helsing picked up the keys from the hall table, and said: "You copied the plans, Jonathan. Take us to the chapel."

The Professor opened the small oak[3] door. There was a terrible smell of old air, fresh blood and earth.

"Count the boxes," said Van Helsing.

There were only twenty-nine! While searching, I saw Quincey step suddenly back from one corner. We watched and saw a mass of phosphorescence[4], twinkling[5] like stars. Then the whole place filled with rats. Arthur, who seemed prepared, rushed to a door and opened it. Taking out a silver whistle, he blew it; three dogs came running in. With the arrival of the dogs all the rats vanished.

We searched the whole house, and found a receipt[6] left by Mr Joseph Smollet, a carrier[7], from Walworth.

As dawn came, we left. Van Helsing took the front-door key off the bunch[8] of keys, locked the door and kept the key.

When I came back to our room, I found Mina sleeping. She looked paler than usual.

Mina Harker's Journal

1 October. Last night, after the men left, I wasn't sleepy. I looked out of the window and saw a thin white mist creeping[9] over the grass.

I went to bed, but got up again to look out. The mist was thicker, lying against the house, as if climbing up to the windows.

I had a strange dream. I couldn't move, and fog had filled the room, covering everything with heavy, cold air. The fog turned into a column[10], and the red of the gaslight on the wall turned into two red eyes.

The last thing I remember was a white face bending over me.

1 revolver [rɪˋvɑlvɚ] (n.) 左輪手槍
2 skeleton key 萬用鑰匙
3 oak [ok] (a.) 橡樹製的
4 phosphorescence [ˏfɑsfəˋrɛsn̩s] (n.) 磷光
5 twinkle [ˋtwɪŋkl̩] (v.) 閃閃發光
6 receipt [rɪˋsit] (n.) 收據
7 carrier [ˋkærɪɚ] (n.) 運送人
8 bunch [bʌntʃ] (n.) 串
9 creep [krip] (v.) 爬行
10 column [ˋkɑləm] (n.) 圓柱

Chapter 20

61 Jonathan Harker's Journal

1 October, evening. Visited Joseph Smollet in Walworth.

He remembered going to Carfax and moving the missing boxes. He said that six were left at 197 Chicksand Lane, Mile End, and six at Jamaica Lane, Bermondsey. He is inquiring[1] about the others.

Mina is fast asleep, and looks very pale. I expect she is worried.

2 October, evening. This morning Smollet told me a Mr Bloxam had moved nine boxes to a Piccadilly address; he described the house. I went to Piccadilly and located it easily. After much research I eventually[2] found out that a foreign nobleman called Count de Ville was the owner of 347 Piccadilly.

Boxes

- Why do you think all the boxes are in different houses?
- Who is Count de Ville?

1 inquire [ɪnˋkwaɪr] (v.) 詢問
2 eventually [ɪˋvɛntʃuəlɪ] (adv.) 最後；終於

Chapter 21

62 Dr Seward's Diary

3 October. Last night, a mental patient who lived at the asylum had an accident. His name was Renfield. Renfield's skull[1] was fractured[2] and his back broken. When Van Helsing arrived, we relieved the pressure[3] on Renfield's brain, hoping he could then talk. Arthur and Quincey joined us.

Renfield's eyes opened and he said: "I have had a terrible dream."

Then Van Helsing said in a quiet, serious tone: "Tell us your dream, Mr Renfield.'

"No," said Renfield. "It was not a dream. It was terribly real." He paused and then continued. "He came to the window in a mist like he always does. The first time he was solid[4] and his eyes were bright and angry. He was laughing with his red mouth and sharp white teeth. Then he promised me things so I invited him in. He slid[5] in through the cracks[6] in the window. But tonight he didn't stay with me – he went after somebody else. I was angry because I wanted him to stay with me. I grabbed[7] the mist tight, but his eyes burned me and I let go. He lifted me up and threw me down, and the mist flowed[8] away under the door."

"We know the worst now," said Van Helsing. "It may not be too late. Let us warn the Harkers! We need all our arms[9] – there is not a moment to spare[10]!"

Van Helsing turned the door handle[11] of the Harkers's door. It did not open. We threw ourselves against it. With a crash it burst[12] open.

The moonlight shone brightly through the window and lit up a terrible scene in front of our eyes.

Jonathan was lying on the bed. Kneeling on the side of the bed, dressed in white, was Mina. A black figure stood beside her. It was the Count. He was holding her face against his chest with his hand, forcing her to drink blood. Her white nightshirt was covered in blood.

When we burst into the room, the Count's eyes flamed red, and his sharp, white teeth moved like an animal's. He threw Mina back and jumped towards us.

Van Helsing held up his envelope of holy wafer. The Count stopped and moved backwards. We all lifted our crucifixes and advanced towards him.

The moon went behind a cloud, and when Quincey turned on the gaslight, we saw a faint mist going under the door.

1 skull [skʌl] (n.) 頭蓋骨
2 fracture [ˋfræktʃɚ] (v.) 破裂
3 pressure [ˋprɛʃɚ] (n.) 壓力
4 solid [ˋsɑlɪd] (a.) 固體的
5 slide [slaɪd] (v.) 滑（動詞三態：slide; slid; slid, slidden）
6 crack [kræk] (n.) 裂縫
7 grab [græb] (v.) 抓取
8 flow [flo] (v.) 流出
9 arms [ɑrmz] (n.)〔複〕武器
10 spare [spɛr] (v.) 騰出（時間）
11 handle [ˋhændḷ] (n.) 把手
12 burst [bɝst] (v.) 爆炸（動詞三態：burst; burst, bursted; burst, bursted）

The Mist

- What is the mist?
- Make a list of the ways Dracula appears in the story.

Arthur and Quincey went to search for him.

When Arthur returned he said: "I could not see him anywhere, and he has destroyed the manuscripts[1] and phonograph[2] recordings."

"Thank goodness there is another copy in the safe!" I interrupted.

"Downstairs there was no sign of him," Arthur continued, "so I went to Renfield's room. The poor fellow is dead. What about you, Quincey?"

"I went outside and saw a bat rise from Renfield's window and fly westwards. I expected to see him go into Carfax, but he obviously[3] went to another hiding place. The sky is already red in the east."

Van Helsing spoke to Mina.

1 manuscript [ˋmænjə͵skrɪpt] (n.) 手稿；原稿
2 phonograph [ˋfonə͵græf] (n.) 留聲機
3 obviously [ˋɑbvɪəslɪ] (adv.) 顯然地

65 "The Count came into my room," she said. "He wanted to kill Jonathan if I was not quiet, then he sucked my blood. I felt compelled[1] to let him. Then he got angry with me because I was helping you all. As my punishment[2] he forced me to drink his blood from a cut that he made in his chest[3]."

Mina

- What has happened to Mina?
- What is she now in danger of becoming?
- Do you think the others can save her?

Chapter 22

66 Jonathan Harker's Journal

3 October. We met at 6:30. Van Helsing had a plan. He wanted us to find all of the Count's boxes and sterilize[4] them with holy wafers. That way the Count could not use them.

Before Van Helsing left he placed some things in Mina's room to stop Dracula from entering. Then he placed a wafer on her forehead to protect her against the Count. There was a terrible scream as the wafer burned Mina as soon as it touched her skin.

I left with a heavy heart. First, we went into Carfax and we sterilized the boxes there. Next we decided to go to the Piccadilly house. We went to central London by train and found a locksmith[5] to help us get in. There was a terrible smell inside. We found eight boxes in the dining room, and we put a piece of holy wafer in each.

However, one box was missing, and to finish our work we needed to find it. The rest of the house was empty. On a table there were documents for the houses in Piccadilly, Bermondsey and Mile End, and some keys. Arthur and Quincey took the keys and left to sterilize the boxes in Bermondsey and Mile End. The two doctors and I waited for their return – or for the coming of the Count.

1 compel [kəm`pɛl] (v.) 強迫
2 punishment [`pʌnɪʃmənt] (n.) 懲罰
3 chest [tʃɛst] (n.) 胸口
4 sterilize [`stɛrə,laɪz] (v.) 淨化；消毒
5 locksmith [`lɑk,smɪθ] (n.) 鎖匠

Chapter 23

67 Dr Seward's Diary

3 October. A telegraph boy brought a message: "12:45. Look out for D. He has left Carfax now and gone south. Mina."

Soon, Arthur and Quincey arrived. They had sterilized the other boxes.

"He will be here soon," said Van Helsing. "Have all your arms ready."

We were all in position when we heard the key turn in the lock. But the Count was prepared. He jumped into the room, getting past us before we could move. Harker blocked the other door and struck at his heart with his long knife, but the Count was too quick. The knife cut his coat, and banknotes[1] and gold coins fell out.

I moved forward, with the crucifix and wafer in my hand, seeing the monster move backwards. The others did the same, but the Count threw himself under Harker's knife before he could strike. He grabbed some money from the floor, dashed[2] across the room and jumped through the window.

We ran to it, saw him climb up the steps and across the yard. He opened the stable[3] door and turned, saying: "You think you can beat me! You will all be sorry for this! You think I have no place to rest, but I have. Your girls are already mine, and soon you will be mine, too!"

He went into the stable, locking the door behind him.

We moved into the hall, and the Professor spoke: "He fears us, and he fears time. Why was he in such a hurry? Why did he take the money? Follow him quickly. I will stay here and make sure he can use nothing if he returns."

The Professor put the remaining money and house documents into his pockets. Arthur and Quincey soon returned. They found no trace of Dracula. It was nearly sunset, so with sad hearts we came back to my house, where Mrs Harker was waiting for us. After supper, the Professor prepared the Harkers' room against the coming of the Vampire.

Jonathan Harker's Journal

4 October, early morning. Mina woke me, saying: "Call the Professor. He must hypnotize me before dawn. I feel that I will be able to speak freely then."

He arrived and quickly moved his hands around her head. When Mina was hypnotized, he asked: "Where are you now?"

1 banknote [ˋbæŋknot] (n.) 鈔票
2 dash [dæʃ] (v.) 急奔
3 stable [ˋstebḷ] (n.) 馬廄

"It is dark," she said. "I can hear water moving outside."

"Are you on a ship?" he asked.

"Yes! I can hear footsteps overhead, and the sound of chains[1]."

"What are you doing?"

"I am still as death," answered Mina.

Her eyes closed as the sun rose.

"Now we know what was in the Count's mind. He wanted to escape and we must follow," said the Professor. "But first let us rest. We are safe, because there is water between him and us which he cannot cross."

"But why do we need to follow him, now he has gone?" asked Mina.

"Because, my dear Madam Mina," said Van Helsing, "he can live for centuries, and you are a mortal[2] woman. Time is important now, because his mark is on your throat."

1 chain [tʃen] (n.) 鏈條
2 mortal [ˋmɔrtl̩] (a.) 會死的
3 characteristic [ˏkærəktəˋrɪstɪk] (n.) 特徵

Chapter 24

70 Mina Harker's Journal

5 October, 5 p.m. This is the situation: the Count is returning to Transylvania by ship. The only ship that left for the Black Sea between today and yesterday was the Czarina Catherine. The Count and his box are on board and on their way to Varna.

Dr Seward's Diary

5 October. Van Helsing said: "Madam Mina is changing, and we must be prepared. The characteristics[3] of the vampire are in her face – sharper teeth and harder eyes. I fear the Count can read her mind."

I nodded my agreement.

"We must not tell her our plans," he went on, "so she has nothing to tell him."

Chapter 25

71 Dr Seward's Diary

11 October. At sunset yesterday Mina said: "I know I will change like Lucy. Please promise me that you will drive a stake through me and cut off my head."

We all took her hand and promised.

Then she continued: "That time, if it comes, will perhaps come quickly and without warning. You must act immediately. At such a time I will be your enemy[1]."

28 October. We left England on the twelfth, traveling across land by train, and got to Varna on the fifteenth to await the *Czarina Catherine*. But today we received a telegram saying the ship was entering Galatz, a port[2] on the Danube.

Van Helsing fears that the Count read Mina's mind, and knew we were in Varna, and so changed his travel plans to escape from us.

1 enemy [ˋɛnəmɪ] (n.) 敵人
2 port [port] (n.) 港口

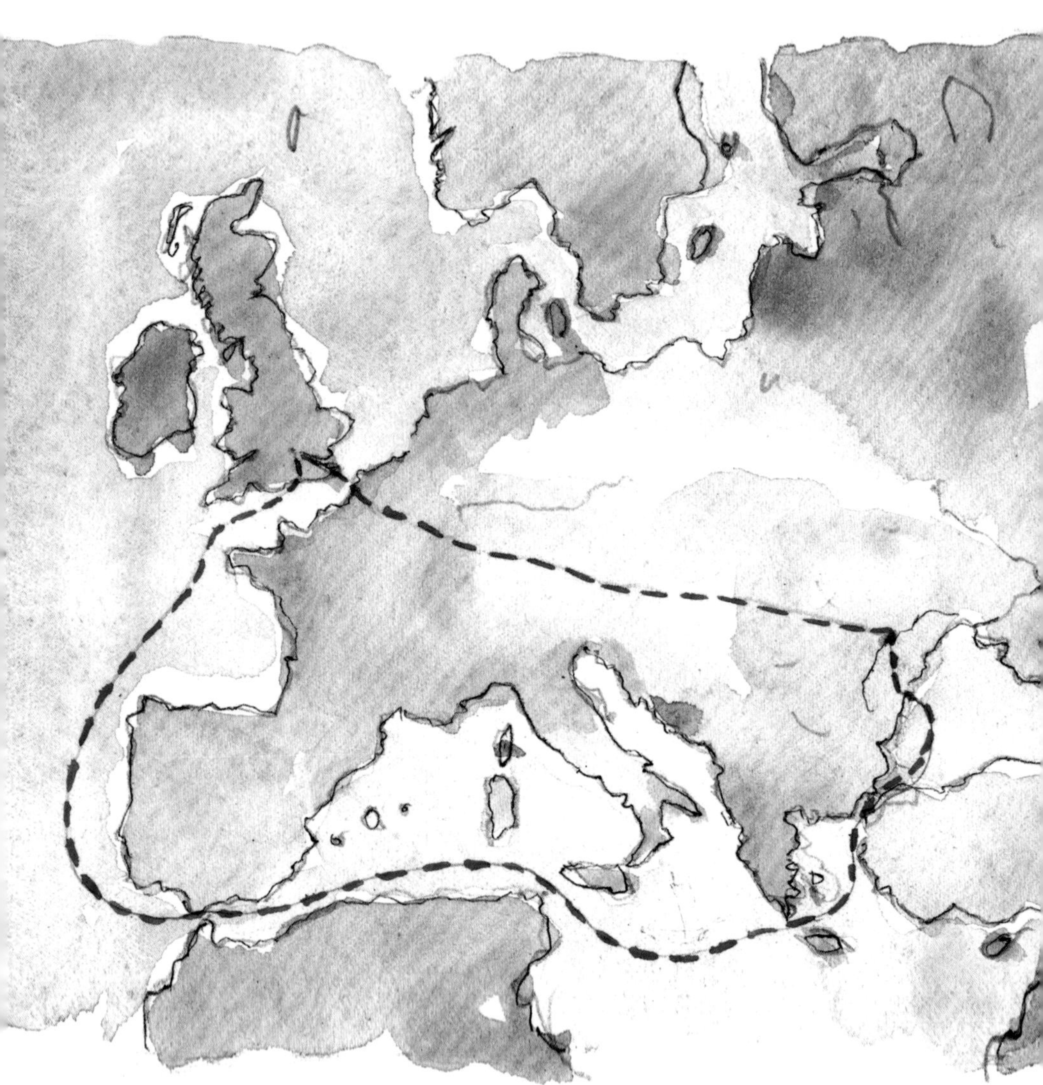

Chapter 26

72 Jonathan Harker's Journal

30 October. We visited the *Czarina Catherine*. We discovered that the box was delivered to a man called Skinsky. However, while we were talking, a man arrived saying that Skinsky was dead. His throat was torn open as if by a wild animal!

Mina has examined the maps and believes the box is being taken by boat to join the River Bistritza which flows round the Borgo Pass, the nearest place to Dracula's castle.

We decided that Arthur and I will travel down the river in a fast steamboat[1], while Quincey and Seward will ride along the bank on horses. Meanwhile, Van Helsing and Mina will travel by train to Veresti, then by carriage to Castle Dracula.

1 steamboat [ˋstimbot] (n.) 汽船；輪船

Chapter 27

73 Memorandum by Abraham Van Helsing

4 November. To John Seward, of Purfleet, London, in case I do not see him again.

I am writing by a fire. It is extremely cold, and it will soon snow. Madam Mina sleeps all the time. We reached the Borgo Pass after sunrise yesterday. I hypnotized Mina and she said: "Darkness and the moving of water."

We started up the byroad[1]. At sunset I was unable to hypnotize Madam Mina. I lit a fire, and she cooked some food for me, but she wasn't hungry. She stared at me with bright eyes. When she is asleep she looks increasingly healthy. It frightens me.

5 November, morning. Yesterday, we camped[2] below the castle. I drew a ring around Madam Mina in the snow and spread crumbled[3] holy wafer round it.

"Come here," I said, testing her.

She stopped after one step. "I cannot," she said.

1 byroad [ˋbaɪˏrod] (n.) 小道
2 camp [kæmp] v.) 紮營
3 crumbled [ˋkrʌmbḷd] (a.) 弄碎的

74 Later it started snowing, and I could see three figures of women whirling[1] in the mist. I wanted to put more wood on the fire, but Madam Mina said: "Stay inside the ring. Here you are safe."

The whirling figures came closer, but they never entered the circle. Then they materialized[2] into the three women that Jonathan saw in the castle. They pointed at Madam Mina.

"Come, sister, come to us!" they said in sweet voices.

There was horror in Madam Mina's eyes. I was happy because it means she is not yet one of them.

Dr Seward's Diary

5 November. At dawn we saw some gypsies moving away from the river with a large cart. Snow is falling lightly and wolves are howling.

Dr Van Helsing's Memorandum

5 November, afternoon. I left Madam Mina in the holy circle, and went to the castle alone. I soon found the old chapel and saw the three women lying in their vampire sleep. They were so beautiful that I almost lost my nerve[3]. I delayed as I gazed[4] at them almost as if I was paralyzed[5]. But then I thought of Madam Mina, and I nerved myself to my work.

I searched all the tombs in the chapel and found only these three Undead phantoms. Another, bigger tomb had just one word on it:

This was the Undead home of the King-Vampire. I laid some holy wafer in it, to keep him out forever. Then I began my terrible task. The screeching[6] and writhing[7] of the three women was terrible as the stakes went into their bodies, but in each one I saw the happiness in their faces as their souls were won back. As my knife finished cutting off each head, the whole body crumbled away into dust.

When I stepped into the circle where Madam Mina slept, she woke up and said: "Let us go to meet my husband. He is coming."

1 whirl [hwɝl] (v.) 旋轉
2 materialize [məˋtɪrɪəl͵aɪz] (v.) 使具體化
3 nerve [nɝv] (n.) 膽量
4 gaze [gez] (v.) 凝視
5 paralyze [ˋpærə͵laɪz] (v.) 使癱瘓
6 screech [skritʃ] (v.) 發出尖銳刺耳的聲音
7 writhe [raɪð] (v.) 扭動；翻滾

76 Mina Harker's Journal

6 November. The Professor and I started walking in the direction[1] that I knew Jonathan was coming from. We could hear wolves howling in the distance.

I was tired and the Professor found a protected place under a large rock and made a bed of furs for me. He then took out his binoculars[2] and searched the horizon[3].

Suddenly he shouted: "Look! Madam Mina! Look!"

I saw gypsies on horses pulling a large cart. On the cart was a great square box and I was afraid when I saw it. While I was looking, the Professor drew a ring around us and crumbled some holy wafer around it.

"At least you will be safe from him here!" he said. He looked again.

"They are moving fast to get there before sunset." Then he shouted again: "Look! Quincey and Seward are coming from the south!"

I took the glasses and looked. I saw the two men. Then I saw Jonathan and Arthur approaching fast from the north side. I told the Professor and he shouted happily: "They are all converging[4]. We will have the gypsies covered on all sides."

He took out his Winchester[5] and I got my pistol[6]. Through the binoculars I saw wolves gathering from all directions.

1 direction [dəˋrɛkʃən] (n.) 方向
2 binoculars [bɪˋnɑkjələ˞z] (n.) 〔複〕雙筒望遠鏡
3 horizon [həˋraɪzn̩] (n.) 地平線
4 converge [kənˋvɝdʒ] (v.) 會合
5 Winchester [ˋwɪntʃɪstə˞] (n.) 溫徹斯特式連發來福槍
6 pistol [ˋpɪstl̩] (n.) 手槍

Finale

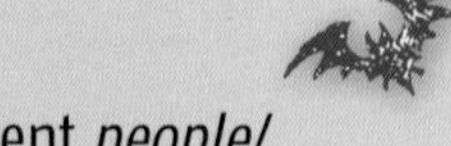

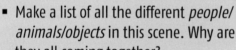

- Make a list of all the different *people/ animals/objects* in this scene. Why are they all coming together?
- Do you think this is an exciting finale?

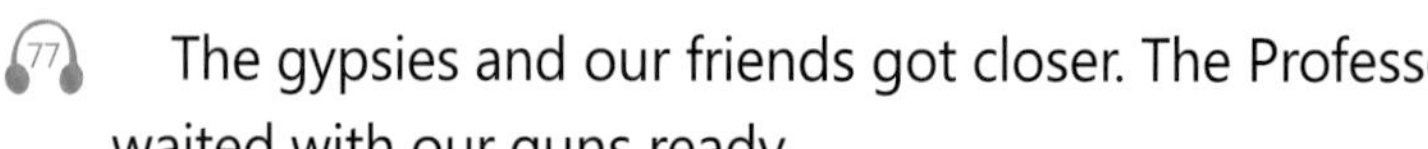

The gypsies and our friends got closer. The Professor and I waited with our guns ready.

Suddenly, Jonathan and Quincey shouted: "Halt[1]!"

The gypsy leader ordered his companions to proceed[2]. But the four men raised their rifles[3] and ordered them to stop.

The gypsies quickly surrounded[4] the cart and pointed their knives and guns at us.

Jonathan and Quincey were determined to finish their task before the sun went down. Jonathan jumped onto the cart, and with his big knife, began taking the lid off the box. Quincey arrived to help at the other side; his hand was holding a stomach[5] wound. The top of the box soon came off.

The gypsies gave in[6]. The sun was almost down on the mountain tops by now. The Count lay in the box on the earth, his red eyes glaring[7] as they saw the sinking[8] sun. There was a look of triumph in them.

Sunset

- Why is it so important to kill the Count before sunset?

Then Jonathan's great knife flashed[9] as it cut through the Count's throat, and at the same moment, Quincey's knife plunged[10] into his heart. With incredible[11] speed, Dracula's whole body crumbled into dust. And at that moment, a look of peace crossed the Count's face.

The gypsies turned without a word and rode away, and the wolves followed.

At this point Quincey Morris fell to the ground, blood still pouring through his fingers. I ran to him, and so did the two doctors. He took my hand and smiled at me.

"I am happy to have been of service," he said. "It was worth dying for."

And to our bitter grief[12], he died.

1 halt [hɔlt] (v.) 停止
2 proceed [prəˋsid] (v.) 繼續進行
3 rifle [ˋraɪfḷ] (n.) 步槍；來福槍
4 surround [səˋraʊnd] (v.) 圍繞
5 stomach [ˋstʌmək] (n.) 胃；腹部
6 give in 放棄
7 glare [glɛr] (v.) 怒視
8 sink [sɪŋk] (v.) 下沉（動詞三態：sink; sank, sunk; sunk, sunken）
9 flash [flæʃ] (v.) 閃光
10 plunge [plʌndʒ] (v.) 刺進
11 incredible [ɪnˋkrɛdəbḷ] (a.) 難以置信的
12 grief [grif] (n.) 悲傷；不幸

NOTE

Seven years ago we all went through hell. The happiness some of us have enjoyed since then is, we think, worth the pain we experienced. It is an added joy to Mina and I that our son, Quincey, has his birthday on the same day that Quincey Morris died.

In the summer of this year we made a journey to Transylvania, and went to some of the places which are full of terrible memories. It was almost impossible to believe the things we saw and heard were true. The castle still stood high above the desolate[1] forests and mountains.

Arthur and Seward are both also happily married. When I took all the papers out of the safe, where they were put years ago, apart from[2] the later notebooks and Van Helsing's memorandum[3], I realized it was all a mass[4] of typed pages, and not one authentic[5] document to prove any of the story.

Van Helsing summed it up: "We don't need proof[6], and we don't ask anyone to believe us. Your little boy Quincey will some day know what a brave woman his mother is. He already knows her sweetness and loving care; later on he will understand how some men loved her so much, that they risked[7] everything for her sake[8]."

Jonathan Harker

1 desolate [ˋdɛsḷət] (a.) 荒蕪的
2 apart from 除……之外
3 memorandum [͵mɛməˋrændəm] (n.) 備忘錄
4 mass [mæs] (n.) 大量
5 authentic [ɔˋθɛntɪk] (a.) 可信的
6 proof [pruf] (n.) 物證
7 risk [rɪsk] (v.) 冒險
8 for one's sake 為了某人的緣故

After Reading

A Personal Response

1. Work with a partner. Discuss what you liked most and least about the story.

2. Did you like the end of the story? Did you guess the ending before you finished reading?

3. How was the story similar and different to any films and books you know about vampires?

4. Do you think that vampires like Dracula really exist? Why? Why not?

5. "*Dracula* is a story where love is the most important thing." Discuss this idea in a group of four.

6. Is there anything you would like to change in the story? If so, what is it and why?

7. Who do you think is the hero of the story, and why?

8. Which character would you like to be and why?

B Comprehension

9 Tick true (T) or false (F).

T F ⓐ Count Dracula doesn't really die at the end of the story.

T F ⓑ Jonathan Harker helps Count Dracula to buy a house.

T F ⓒ Lucy Westenra changes into a vampire.

T F ⓓ Mina goes to Bucharest when Jonathan is in hospital.

T F ⓔ Count Dracula changes into a wolf to jump off the *Demeter* in Whitby.

T F ⓕ Van Helsing is an expert on unusual illnesses.

T F ⓖ Dr Seward gets killed at the end of the story.

10 Write the numbers 1-6 on the lines to put these events in order.

____ ⓐ The men find Count Dracula's boxes of earth in his London houses.

____ ⓑ Dr Seward invites Professor Van Helsing to London to help.

____ ⓒ The *Demeter* arrives at Whitby harbor.

____ ⓓ Count Dracula starts sucking Mina Harker's blood.

____ ⓔ Van Helsing and the other men watch Lucy in the cemetery.

____ ⓕ Lucy Westenra starts to lose blood regularly.

11 Van Helsing tells us a lot about vampires. Answer these questions.

(a) What special things does he say that vampires can do?
(b) What limitations do vampires have?
(c) How can vampires be defeated?

12 How many vampires are defeated or put to rest in the story?

13 When and where does Count Dracula appear in the following ways?

(a) as a large bat
(b) as a white mist
(c) as a large dog (or wolf)

14 When and where do hundreds of rats appear?

15 Answer these questions about the three vampire women in Dracula's castle.

(a) When do they appear and who to?
(b) What do they look like?
(c) Why does Count Dracula get angry with them?
(d) What happens to them at the end of the story?

C Characters

16 What is the name of these characters, and what part do they play in the story?

a) The man who sent Jonathan Harker to Transylvania.

____

b) Arthur's American friend.

____

c) The patient in the mental asylum who let Dracula in.

____

d) The person who looked after Dracula's boxes in Whitby.

____

17 Make a list of the good characters in the book. Who do you like the most, and which the least? Explain your reasons to a partner.

18 Write a paragraph describing Count Dracula. Include his physical features and what you know about his character.

19 Who says the following things? Who do they say them to, and what situation do they refer to?

ⓐ You may go anywhere in the castle, except where the doors are locked.
Who?
Who to?
Situation:

ⓑ His red eyes! They are just the same.
Who?
Who to?
Situation:

ⓒ Do not let her out of your sight. You must not sleep all night.
Who?
Who to?
Situation:

ⓓ Most corpses do not look like this. She is Undead.
Who?
Who to?
Situation:

ⓔ You think I have no place to rest, but I have. Your girls are already mine, and soon you will be mine, too.
Who?
Who to?
Situation:

ⓕ I know I will change like Lucy.
Who?
Who to?
Situation:

D Plot and Theme

20 Write what you remember about the following. Then share with a friend.

- a The landlady of the hotel in Bristriz.
- b The blue flames.
- c The reason why Jonathan Harker comes to Transylvania.
- d The Count's castle.
- e The three "ladies".
- f The boxes of earth filled by the gypsies.
- g The *Demeter* arriving at Whitby.
- h Mina and Lucy's friendship.
- i Lucy's sleepwalking.
- j The marks on Lucy's neck.
- k Garlic and crucifixes.
- l The children on Hampstead Heath.
- m The Westenra tomb.
- n The missing boxes of earth in England.
- o The Holy Communion wafers.
- p The journey to Varna.
- q The end of Count Dracula

21 Work in groups of four. Discuss the statements below. Which one(s) best reflect(s) the main theme of *Dracula*?

- a It is important for good to defeat evil.
- b Friendship and collaboration is the most important thing in life.
- c Equality between the sexes is important for success in society.

22 "Count Dracula fails. Why?" Discuss your ideas with a partner.

23 Think about the structure of the novel and answer these questions.

a *Dracula* is an epistolary novel. What types of texts are used to tell the story?
b Which character in the story puts all the material together?
c How many different characters help to tell the story?
d Do you like this way of telling a story?

24 Fill in the table with the best moments of the story to show examples of the following things. Then compare your answers with a partner.

Adventure	
Horror	
Romance	
Tragedy	

25 Do you think the story is realistic? Think about the following.

a Are there parts of the story where Bram Stoker expects us to believe too much?
b Are there too many problems which are too easily solved?
c Do things which seem impossible for human beings happen?

E Language

26 Complete these sentences from the story with the prepositions in the box.

in front of beside into in to on at over

a I lay .... an old sofa and looked out at the moonlit view.

b I realized that I have always been in danger and now I am afraid .... night.

c The white sandy road stretched .... us.

d Last night I went back .... the room.

e I shall try to crawl .... to his window.

f I got .... the carriage.

g Suddenly four coal-black horses appeared .... our coach.

h Let me warn you not to fall asleep .... other parts of the castle.

27 Using some of the prepositions from Exercise **26** (and others), write a sentence about each of the different places where the story of *Dracula* is set.

Transylvania Whitby London Exeter Purfleet Varna

28 Underline the prepositions used in these sentences about places which are described in *Dracula*.

a I opened another door into a ruined chapel.

b We stopped in front of a huge, dark, ruined castle.

c He carried my luggage up a winding stair, along a stone passage and opened a heavy door.

d Whitby is lovely with the immense Abbey ruins.

29 What do the prepositions help to create in the sentences? Write two sentences about *Dracula* using some of these prepositions. Read your sentences to a partner.

30 Make questions and answers using will.

(a) Where / Dracula's / carriage / meet / Jonathan Harker / ?
Q: ______________________________
A: ______________________________

(b) How long / Jonathan / stay / at the Count's castle / ?
Q: ______________________________
A: ______________________________

(c) Why / Lucy / die / ?
Q: ______________________________
A: ______________________________

(d) How / Van Helsing / change / Lucy / from Undead to dead / ?
Q: ______________________________
A: ______________________________

(e) How / Van Helsing / find / Count Dracula / ?
Q: ______________________________
A: ______________________________

(f) What / Van Helsing / do / to kill / Count Dracula / ?
Q: ______________________________
A: ______________________________

31 Work with a partner. Use the map to describe how they will catch Count Dracula. Remember to use will.

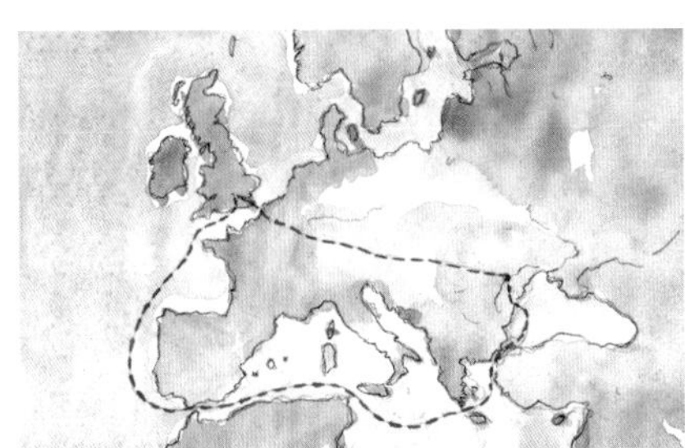

TEST

80 **1** Listen and tick the correct picture.

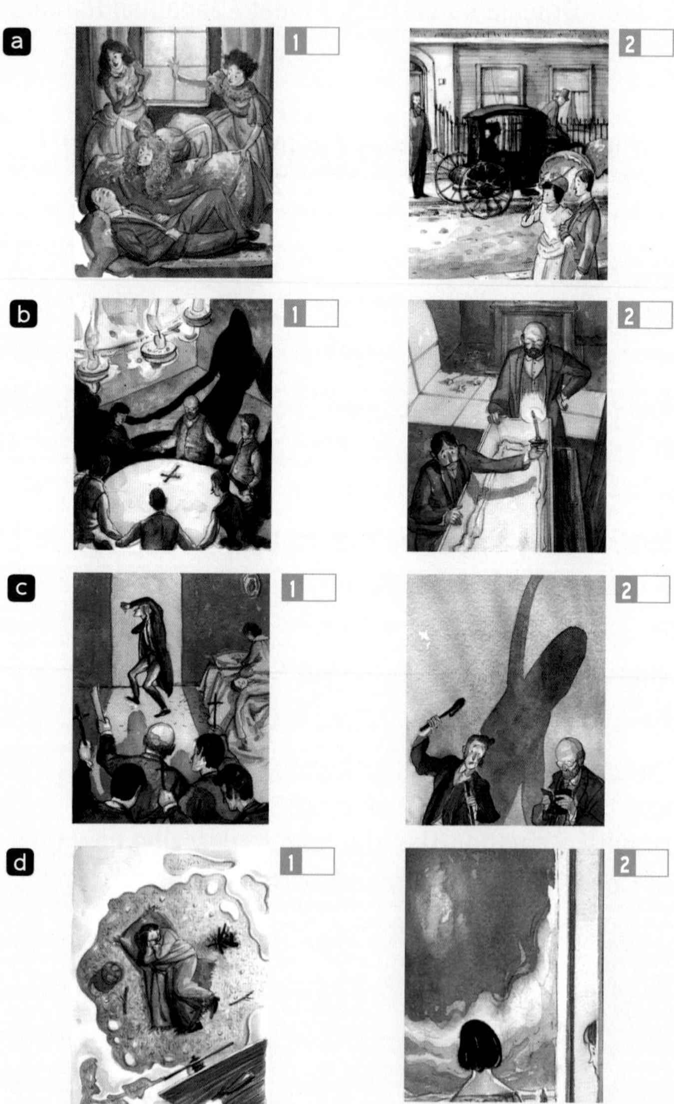

2 Look at this picture from the book. With a partner imagine you are two of the people on the shore. Talk about what has happened.

3 Read the text on page 42 describing the arrival of the *Demeter.* Write an entry for a blog saying what happened.

PROJECT WORK

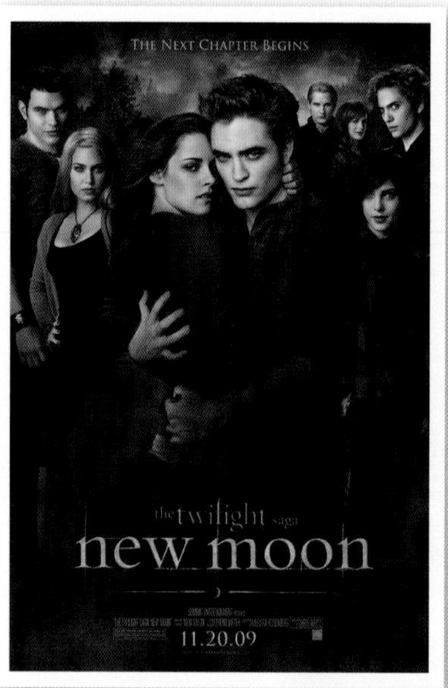

Vampires

Vampires are mythological beings who feed on other humans. Vampire stories date back as far as prehistoric times and are part of many different cultures.

In groups make a vampire magazine, focusing on the following topics:

Vampire Tales

- Meaning of the word "vampire"
- What are vampires?
- How can you defeat vampires?
- The history of vampires
- *Dracula*
- Famous vampires in the past
- Vampires in literature
- Vampires on film and TV

作者簡介

布拉姆・斯托克，1847 年出生於愛爾蘭的都柏林，父親是公務人員。他小時候體弱多病，但在進了都柏林三一學院主修數學之後，轉而擅長體育活動。

1870 年，布拉姆也開始從事公職，不過他最大的興趣是戲劇。他很關注當時代偉大演員亨利・艾爾文爵士的戲劇生涯，1878 年，艾爾文找他擔任倫敦蘭心大戲院的業務經理。同年，他娶了法蘭西絲・巴肯為妻，並於隔年生下獨子艾爾文・諾爾。

在職涯的初期，他在報刊雜誌上發表劇場評論和一些短篇小說，到 1890 年，出版了他第一本的哥德式恐怖小說《蛇跡》（The Snake's Pass），讓他在倫敦的藝文界打開了名氣，並且與多位知名作家成為熟識。

他也曾和艾爾文爵士出國旅行，他特別喜歡去美國，曾經兩次造訪白宮，並和美國總統會面。1897 年，他出版了《吸血鬼德古拉》，這本書讓他真正揚名立萬、廣受歡迎。

艾爾文爵士於 1905 年過世，布拉姆還為他寫了傳記。在這期間，布拉姆也曾經中風一次，病癒之後，繼續執筆寫作，直至 1912 年辭世。

本書簡介

《吸血鬼德古拉》（1897 年）的故事場景設定在羅馬尼亞的川夕凡尼亞、英國的倫敦、愛塞特、惠特比，以及黑海旁邊的瓦爾納和古拉茲。這本書以「書信體」的方式寫成，也就是說，書中的多位角色是透過期刊、日記、信件、電報、報紙文章和航海日誌，來呈現劇中人物各自的故事陳述。

在故事中，年輕的英國律師強納生．哈克，他前往川夕凡尼亞的古堡拜訪德古拉伯爵，為他說明在倫敦置產的事宜。哈克在那裡遭遇了恐怖的經歷，得知了古堡裡的德古拉和三位女子都是吸血鬼。

德古拉搬到英國後，哈克和年輕的妻子米娜捲入了這場生死追逐戰，趁為時未晚之前抓住並制止了德古拉。

這篇故事是一部經典的恐怖冒險小說，最後的結局是「邪不勝正」。這本小說也帶出了「現代性」的主題，這在當時代是一個很重要的議題。

在維多利亞時代產生了很多變遷，很多人認為社會無法因應變化。也有人把《吸血鬼德古拉》視為是一種「侵略」小說——一位邪惡的外國人入侵了大英帝國，他會殺害每一個人，把他們都變成吸血鬼，除非有人能夠出來阻止他。

這篇故事也處理了男性與女性之間的關係。有些學者認為德古拉這個角色可能是以瓦拉嘉（位於現在的羅馬尼亞）的弗拉德三世為原型，一般人稱他為 Dracula。Dracula 這個字由 dragon 轉變而來。

第一章

P. 15

本章，我們碰到了從倫敦來的年輕律師強納生・哈克，得知了他要去川夕凡尼亞的德古拉伯爵古堡。

強納生・哈克的日記

5 月 3 日，畢斯崔茲　我途經慕尼黑、維也納和布達佩斯，正在前往川夕凡尼亞的路上。我的感覺就是我走出了西方，來到了東方世界。我的客戶德古拉伯爵，就住在川夕凡尼亞、莫達維亞和布科維納三國的交界處，位於喀爾巴阡山脈的中央，這裡感覺像是歐洲最荒涼、最鮮為人知的地方。我找不到精確標示出這個地方的地圖，只找到附近一個叫做畢斯崔茲的城鎮。

我搭火車一路前進，當我望向窗外時，可以看到一些小鎮和矗立在陡坡上的城堡，還有廣闊的河川和溪流。鄉間的景色很美麗，只是顯得很陌生。

在我抵達畢斯崔茲的旅館後，旅館已經收到了一封要給我的信：

P. 16

> 我的朋友：
>
> 歡迎您！我期待和您見面。
>
> 明天三點，我在駛往布科維納的馬車上為您預留了位子。沿途會經過波戈隘口，我的馬車會在那裡等您，帶您前來。
>
> 您的朋友，
>
> 德古拉

5 月 4 日　在離開旅館時，我打聽了一下德古拉伯爵的事，結果老闆和老闆娘只是在胸前劃了個十字，不肯透露。

老闆娘說：「一定得去嗎？哈克先生，你一定得去嗎？今天是聖喬治節前夕，今晚午夜過後，塵世所有的惡靈都會跑出來。」

接著她取下她頸子上的十字架項鍊，讓我戴上。我感到害怕。

P. 17

5 月 5 日，古堡　我待在馬車上，聽到車夫和老闆娘重複說著一些我聽不懂的字眼。我查了一下多語辭典，查到「Ordog」表示撒旦，「Pokol」表示地獄，「stregoica」表示巫婆，「vrolok」和「vlkoslak」，代表狼人或吸血鬼。（我得向我的客戶請教一下）

在我出發時，旅館外的人們都在胸前劃了十字，並伸出兩根指頭指著我。有一名乘客解釋，那種手勢是在保佑我可以抵禦惡魔之眼。

P. 18

馬車飛快駛入喀爾巴阡山脈。車夫只停下來一次，點亮車上的燈。最後，我們終於看到波戈隘口就在前頭，那邊的天空中烏雲盤踞，空氣中瀰漫著一股沉重的壓迫感。我們車上的燈是這裡唯一的燈光。眼前的白色沙石路向前延伸，但並沒有看到要來載我的馬車。

最後，車夫說：「這裡沒有馬車，和我們一起去布科維納吧，哈克先生，您可以明天再過來。」

然而就在車夫話一說完，我們的馬匹就開始嘶鳴、噴氣。突然，四匹漆黑如炭的馬出現在我們的馬車旁邊。駕車的人是個高個子，留著棕色的長鬍鬚，黑色帽子遮住了他的臉。在燈光的照射下，他的眼睛閃著紅色光芒。他的嘴唇很紅，有著一口尖利的牙齒，牙齒白如象牙。

他對車夫說：「我的朋友，你今晚早到了。」

我進入馬車，沒有交談，馬車駛入黑暗之中。外頭很冷，我拉起披風圍住肩膀，並用毛毯蓋住膝蓋。我感到害怕，現在接近午夜，我聽見山上傳來狼嚎。馬匹害怕得發抖，駕車的人卻完全不為所動。這時突然間又變得更冷，落下了白雪，大地很快變成白茫茫的一片，而狼嚎聲也更靠近了。

P. 20

黑暗

- 在這一片黑暗中發生了什麼事？
- 黑暗會讓你聯想到什麼？
- 你怕黑嗎？

接著，我看到黑暗之中透出微弱的藍色火焰。駕車人停下車，然後跳下馬車，朝著藍色火焰走去，消失不見。嚎叫聲愈來愈逼近，這時駕車的人再次出現。馬車繼續前行，但我感覺馬車是在繞圈子，整個感覺就像在做惡夢一般。

駕車人一次又一次地下車。最後一次，他走得更遠些。就在這時，烏雲的後方露出了月亮，我看到有一個狼群正包圍著我們，那些狼露出白牙，吐著紅舌頭。

我大叫了一聲，這時突然看到駕車人就站在路中央，他正揮舞著手臂，好像在推開什麼東西。狼群隨即後退，消失不見。

我們疾馳前進，穿過黑暗，然後在一座陰暗的荒廢大城堡前停了下來。

第二章

P. 21

本章，強納生·哈克進入德古拉伯爵的城堡，對這位神秘客戶略知了一二。

強納生·哈克的日記（續）

5月5日　我站在一座陰暗的大城堡前面等待，不禁開始充滿了各種疑問和恐懼。這是什麼樣的恐怖冒險？菜鳥律師被派到陌生的地方出差，算是常態嗎？我一路老遠跑這一趟，就為了向外國客戶說明如何在倫敦置產？

我看不到門環或門鈴，而巨大的大門這時突然打開，眼前站著一位留著長八字鬍、身材高大的黑衣男子。

「歡迎光臨寒舍！請隨您自己的意進來。」他說。

等我一踏進大門，他便跟我握了握手。他的手好冰，簡直像是死人的手一樣。

「德古拉伯爵？」我問。

「我是德古拉。哈克先生，歡迎！過來吃點東西，好好休息一下。」他回答。

P. 22

他拎著我的行李，走上迴旋梯，沿著石廊前進，然後推開一扇厚重的門。我很開心能看到眼前的房間燈火明亮，桌上還擺著晚餐，而且壁爐裡燃燒著火。那裡還有一間大臥室，也生著火。

「請坐下來用餐。我已經用過晚餐，恕我無法陪您一起用餐。」伯爵說。

用完餐後，我們在壁爐旁聊天，我端詳了他的長相。他鼻梁削瘦，天庭飽滿，

後腦勺的頭髮濃密。他的眉毛很粗，而且幾乎在鼻子上方連成一線；八字鬍底下的嘴巴看起來有點冷酷，在鮮紅的嘴唇中，牙齒顯得很白，而且出奇得尖利。他的耳朵尖尖的，膚色蒼白；他的手掌很寬大，手指很修長，長長的指甲削得很尖；奇怪的是，他的掌心居然長毛。

伯爵靠近我，用手碰了我一下，我突然感到很不舒服。

最後，他說：「您一定累了，您可以盡量睡，我明天下午以前都不在。」

5月7日　我很晚才起床。早餐早已準備好。吃過早餐後，我發現一間擺滿英文書籍的書房！我開始讀這些書，卻在抬頭時突然看到了伯爵。

「很高興你找到我的書房，這些書能帶給我好幾個鐘頭的快樂時光。」他說。

P. 24

「我是否可以隨時來這個書房？」我問。

「當然可以。城堡的任何地方你都可以去，除了那些上鎖的房間。」他回答。

接著，我問他昨天夜裡所看到的藍色火焰。

他說：「有人認為，昨晚是惡靈所統治的夜晚，而且在藏有寶藏的地方會有藍色火焰燃燒。但大部分的人會待在家裡，不敢出門，所以寶藏還是原封不動。」

之後，我們看了一些他倫敦那間房子的文件，因為他想在英國購買一些房地產。我告訴他有一個佔地大、位置偏僻的老莊園，叫作「卡菲莊園」，位在一間精神病療養院的旁邊。

5月8日　我想我在這本日記中寫了太多細節，但我現在卻覺得慶幸，因為寫了這些事件，能幫我打住如脫韁野馬般的幻想。

今天早上，我把刮鬍鏡掛在窗口，正準備刮鬍子時，突然感覺到伯爵的手搭在我的肩膀上。

他說：「早安。」

結果我嚇了一大跳，因為我在鏡子裡沒看到他，我嚇得劃傷了自己的臉。

我轉身回應伯爵，等我又轉過頭來時，我看到鏡子裡頭還是沒有他的身影。我很驚訝，開始感到不安。

P. 25

接著，伯爵看到我臉上的血跡後，他兩眼彷彿噴出怒火一樣，並且伸手抓住我的喉嚨。

我往後一退，當他的手碰到旅館老闆娘的十字架時，表情立刻改變。

「小心您會割傷自己，這個國家比您想像得還要危險。」他說道。然後拿走我的刮鬍鏡，說；「這種東西會惹麻煩，這是在男人的虛榮心之下產生的可怕工具。」

他打開窗戶，把鏡子扔下庭院，砸個粉碎，然後一言不發地離開。

我獨自吃著早餐。我還沒看過伯爵用餐或是喝水，為什麼會這樣？早餐過後，我在城堡裡四處逛逛。我發現一個朝南的房間，那裡窗外的景色十分壯觀，可以看到整片的森林和河谷。我這才意識到，這座城堡位於險峻的斷崖邊——斷崖深達三百公尺！

我又繼續探索，到處是一扇又一扇的門，卻都上了鎖。沒有路可以走出城堡，除了爬窗戶出去。我被關在城堡裡！

第三章

P. 26

本章，強納生・哈克了解到，在城堡裡他是獨自一人，與伯爵和三名年輕「女性」在一起。

強納生・哈克的日記（續）

我看到伯爵為我鋪床，所以這裡也沒有僕人，這讓我感到害怕，因為這表示，在我抵達那天晚上駕車的人是他，控制了狼群的人也是他。

5 月 12 日 昨天晚上，伯爵問我了英國的法律：他能不能在英國的不同地區，擁有兩名以上的律師？

「當然可以。人們常為了不想讓同一個人知道自己所有的業務，會聘請一名以上的律師。」我回答。

他突然又問道：「您來這裡之後，有寫信給您在愛塞特的老闆霍金斯先生或是其他什麼人嗎？」

「沒有，因為我不知道怎麼把信寄出去。」我回答。

「那麼，您就寫信吧，說您會在這裡待一個月。」他說。

「您要我待那麼久？」我問道，心都涼了。

P. 27

「是的，而且請您只寫公事。」他回答。

我知道他想在信寄出前先看過信，所以我就寫了正式信函給霍金斯先生，還有我親愛的女友米娜。伯爵也寫了幾封信，然後離開房間。我看到那些信是要給英國東北部惠特比的某個人、保加利亞瓦爾納的一名德國人，以及倫敦的銀行。

伯爵回來之後，他說：「我今晚得工作。我要提醒你，千萬不要在這座城堡的其他地方睡著了。要趕回來這裡睡覺，這樣你才會安全。」

稍後 我往上走到那個可以一覽南邊景色的房間。我感覺自己像個囚犯一樣。月光亮如白晝。我靠在窗子把頭探出去，竟看到伯爵從樓下的窗戶出來，爬下城牆。他移動的速度很快，像隻蜥蜴一樣。我極度驚恐。

5 月 15 日 我再次目睹伯爵以蜥蜴爬行的方式離開。我探索這座城堡，最後使勁推開一扇門，進入了另一個房間。

月光從窗戶流瀉進來，我在這裡感覺很自在，於是在一張小桌子前坐下來寫這本日記。

P. 29

5 月 16 日 昨晚，我又走去那個房間。在寫完日記後，我覺得很睏。我記得伯爵的警告，但我仍決定在那裡睡覺。我躺在一張舊沙發上，望著窗外的月色。

我猜我睡著了，而我害怕我所目睹的事情會是真的。我看到三名年輕女子，月光從她們背後照過來，但卻沒有看到她們的影子。其中有兩人是黑髮，讓我聯想到伯爵，另一個則留著大波浪金髮，有一對藍眼睛。她們每個人都有一口發亮的貝齒和鮮紅的嘴唇，我一方面感到害怕，一方面卻又想親吻她們。

她們竊竊私語作笑，那種樣子並不像

是人類。那兩名黑髮女子說：「去啊，你先！他又年輕又強壯，夠我們三個親吻。」

我躺著，從睫毛下看到金髮女孩俯在我上方，我能感覺到她的氣息。她像動物那樣的舔拭嘴唇，接著我感覺她的兩顆尖牙抵在我脖子的皮膚上。

就在那一瞬間，我意識到伯爵出現了。伯爵大發雷霆，一把揪住女孩，血紅的眼睛裡怒火熊熊。他把女孩丟到房間的另一頭，對另外兩人舉手示意。在我抵達這裡的那個晚上，他也用相同的手勢制服過狼群。他用低吟的聲音講話，但能聽得很清楚。

P.30

「我已經下過禁令，你們好大的膽子竟敢動他？他是屬於我的。但我答應你們，等我用完他之後，你們就可以盡情地親吻他。現在，給我離開！」

「難道我們今天晚上就一無所獲？」其中一人問道，並指著他丟在地上的那個袋子。袋子在蠕動著，好像裡面裝了什麼活物。

他點點頭。一名女子於是跳上前去，打開袋子。我聽到小孩子哭泣的聲音，接著她們帶著那個可怕的袋子，走進朦朧的月光中，往窗外飛去，消失不見。

恐懼懾住了我，我隨之不省人事。

毛骨悚然

- 在這三名女子的場景中，強納生・哈克目睹哪兩件駭人的事？
- 你喜歡看恐怖電影或鬼故事嗎？跟朋友說個鬼故事。

第四章

P.31

本章，強納生・哈克判斷德古拉伯爵顯然不是人類，而且有許多原因讓他足以畏懼他。

強納生・哈克的日記（續）

我在自己的床上醒來，我想是伯爵帶我來這裡的。

5 月 18 日　白天的時候，我去查看了那個房間，結果房間的門被鎖上了，所以我害怕那並不是一場夢。

6 月 17 日　一些吉普賽人駕著兩輛馬拉的大貨車，載著很多大型的空木箱進到院子裡來。吉普賽人卸下箱子後便離開。

6 月 24 日　昨天晚上，我又跑去觀察伯爵。吉普賽人在某個地方工作著——我能聽到鏟子的聲音。

P.32

稍後，我看到他爬出窗子。在等待他回來的時候，我注意到月光中有一些小點點在飄浮著。小點點在我面前飛舞，幾乎要我把催眠，直到幻化成那天夜裡的三名女子。我一邊尖叫，一邊跑回自己的房間。

這時，我突然聽到有女子在庭院哭泣的聲音。我打開窗戶，她對我吼叫道：「怪物，把孩子還給我！」她說完便狂敲著大門。

我聽見伯爵大聲高喊的聲音，接著是狼群嗥叫回應的聲音，然後院子裡奔進來了一群狼群。女人停止哭泣，狼群舔了舔嘴唇後離開。

我要怎麼逃離這個可怕的夢魘？

6 月 25 日，早晨　我明白了自己一直處在危險之中，我現在很害怕夜晚來臨。我沒有在白天看過伯爵，有可能人們醒來時他在睡覺。我決定要潛入他的房間。我應該從他的窗戶爬進去，我要是失手了，那就永別了，親愛的米娜。

同一日，稍後　我平安歸來了！我脫掉靴子，爬過粗糙的大石壁。伯爵的房間裡空空如也，只有落滿灰塵的家具和一堆金幣。

房間的角落裡有一扇門，門內是黑暗的迴旋梯，通向地下室。我往下走到底，打開另一道門，走進廢棄的禮拜室，那裡面以前是墓室。

P. 33

那裡的地板上放著昨天運來的木箱，而伯爵就躺在其中的一個木箱裡。他看起來並不像死人，但也不像睡著了。他的眼神很冷酷，臉頰有暖色，嘴唇也很紅潤，但是卻沒有呼吸和心跳。

我想在他身上搜出鑰匙，但是他那雙死寂的眼睛流露出極為憤恨的神情，於是我便趕緊離開，爬回自己的房間。

6 月 29 日　今天早上，伯爵說：「明天，我的朋友，我們就要分開了。你要回英國，我也要出門去辦些事情，我們將永遠不會再見面了。吉普賽人還有工作要做，貨車會再回來。我的馬車會載你到波戈隘口，在那裡接駁到畢斯崔茲的大馬車。」

P. 34

我有點疑心，便問：「我為什麼不能今晚就走？」

「因為我的車夫和馬匹出去辦事了。」

「我可以用走的。」

「朋友，如果你不願意，我也不會讓你多待一個鐘頭的。」他和善地微笑道。

我於是跟他走下樓，然而當他打開大門後，外面的狼群一片狂嚎。我知道我無法違背伯爵的意願而先離開。他有這些「盟友」，我無法做出違逆他的事情。

「把門關上吧！我明天早上再走。」我喊道。

他於是用力把門闔上。我不發一語地走回房間。伯爵朝我親吻了一下他自己的手，眼中散發勝利的紅色光芒。

是客人，還是囚犯？

- 強納生．哈克覺得自己像客人，還是像囚犯？
- 是什麼阻止了強納生離開？
- 你覺得伯爵為什麼要把強納生留在城堡裡？

倫敦

- 強納生為什麼會認為伯爵想去倫敦？
- 你覺得在強納生．哈克的時代，倫敦大概會是什麼樣貌？
- 現代的倫敦又是什麼樣貌？

6 月 30 日，早晨　天一亮，我就覺得自己安全了。我衝向樓下大廳，跑到前門，但門被鎖上了。我不顧一切想拿到鑰匙，因此想都不想就衝回樓上，然後爬出我的窗戶，朝伯爵的房間爬過去。

P. 35

我進到房間裡，然後打開門，再次往下走進老舊的禮拜室。伯爵躺著的箱子仍放在相同的地方，但箱子闔上了蓋子，蓋子上的釘子都插上，隨時可以封死。我知道我需要搜伯爵的身找鑰匙，於是我打開蓋子，然後把蓋子靠牆放著。

伯爵的樣子看起來年輕許多，頭髮和鬍鬚的顏色變得更深，嘴唇也比以前更鮮紅。

我沒有找到鑰匙。一想到要幫他遷居倫敦，然後長年飲人們的鮮血為食，就令我抓狂。我想殺了他，於是拿起鏟子，準備對著那張令人憎恨的臉用力一擊。

然而就在這一剎那，他的頭轉動了。他用駭人的眼睛直盯著我，我手裡的鏟子一個歪斜，只打到了他的額頭。接著，箱子的蓋子落下，把他給蓋住看不見了。

P. 36

我緊接著聽到貨車和說話的聲音。吉普賽人來了。我跑回伯爵的房間，打算趁大門被打開的那一刻衝出去。然而，並沒有人進門。

接著，我聽到門被打開、有人在走動的聲音。等到講話聲和腳步聲消逝後，我轉身走回樓下的禮拜室，想著看能不能找到別的出口。但這時突然一陣風襲來，樓梯的門就被關上了。我沒辦法把門打開，於是我再度淪為階下囚。

就在我一邊寫著日記時，我還能聽到吉普賽人在搬動箱子、然後把釘子錘入德古拉那個箱子的聲音。我也能聽到說話聲和腳步聲。我聽到了關門的聲音、轉動鑰匙的聲音、另一扇門被打開又被關上的聲音，還有另一支鑰匙轉動的聲音。我聽到庭院裡的貨車聲和人聲，這時聲音漸漸遠去。

我單獨一個人和這些可怕的女人待在城堡裡，但我不要再待在這裡了。我要帶些金幣，爬牆離開城堡。我會找到出路，離開這個鬼地方！

第五章

P. 38

米娜・墨瑞小姐寫給露西・魏斯頓小姐的信

5月9日

最親愛的露西：

原諒我遲遲沒有回信，教職的生活實在忙碌。親愛的朋友，我好渴望見到你，可以和你盡情地聊天。

我為了強納森在學習速記。等我們結婚後，我會幫他處理事務，所以我也正在練習打字。

我們有時會以速記方式通信，他人在川夕凡尼亞，也用這種方法在寫日記。等我去找你之後，我也要用這種方式寫日記。

我剛收到強納生從川夕凡尼亞寄來的隻字片語。他很好，要在那邊待上一個星期左右。我渴望聽到他所有的消息。造訪陌生的國家一定很棒。十點的鐘聲響了。再見。

你親愛的米娜

友誼

・米娜寫信給誰？
・你寫過信給朋友嗎？
・把你和朋友溝通的各種方法列出來。

第六章

P. 40

米娜・墨瑞的日記

7月24日，惠特比 露西和我在車站碰面，我們開車到她和她母親在新月街的房子。

惠特比風景宜人，有占地寬廣的修道院遺跡和教區禮拜堂，兩者都居高臨下。我坐在毗連教堂的院落，俯瞰小鎮、港口和所有接入大海的水道。

露西跟我說了亞瑟・洪伍的事，他是葛達明勛爵的獨子，他們即將舉行婚禮了。這讓我聽了很感傷，因為我已經有一個月沒有強納生的消息了！

7 月 26 日　霍金斯先生轉寄給我一封強納生的來信，信件非常簡短。

他寫得很正式，並提到他正啟程回家，不過我感覺到有點不對勁。

我也擔心露西，因為她又開始夢遊了。她的母親和我決定，我每天晚上都要把我們的房門鎖上。

P. 41

8 月 3 日　又一個星期過去，還是沒有強納生的消息。我希望他不要出了什麼事。

每天晚上，我都會因為露西在房裡走來走去而被吵醒。她想開門，發現門被鎖上之後，她會去找鑰匙。

8 月 6 日　又三天過去了，還是音訊全無。我希望我能知道信要寄到哪裡去，但自從上次那封信之後，就再沒有人有強納生的消息。

第七章

P. 42

《每日電訊報》剪報

8 月 8 日，惠特比

有史以來規模最大的暴風雨，昨夜突如其來侵襲惠特比。午夜時分，傳來奇怪的聲音，緊接著怒潮洶湧、強風嘶吼，海面上出現大量霧氣往內陸飄移，還有閃電和震動大地的轟隆雷聲。

懸崖頂端新架設的探照燈，對返航漁船發揮了很大的作用，引導船隻安全入港。突然間，雲霧散盡，一片清朗，我們看到一艘縱帆船駛入港口，船舵上綁了一具屍體。在船衝上沙岸時，甲板上出現了一隻體型碩大的狗。狗跳下船，直接奔上懸崖，朝教堂墓園跑去。

這艘船名為「迪麥特號」，從黑海瓦爾納港啟程，準備前往英國海岸，船上載運了裝滿泥土的木箱。惠特比的律師畢林頓先生，正式點收那些箱子。

有人發現迪麥特號的航行日誌，顯示船上似乎發生了一些離奇的恐怖事件。首先，船員感覺船上有個瘦高男子存在，接著，船員一個接著一個地失蹤，最後只剩船長。船長被發現時已經死亡，他手上拿著十字架，整個人被綁在舵輪上。

第八章

P. 44

米娜・墨瑞的日記

8月8日　露西整晚焦躁不安。暴風雨很嚇人，她起床著裝兩次，但我都讓她回床上睡覺。

我們去了港口，看看暴風雨所造成的損害。海上依然一片陰暗，危機四伏。

8月11日，凌晨3點　露西的床上是空的。我跑到外面去找她，看到她穿著睡衣，坐在對面懸崖的長椅上，那是我們常去坐的地方。

我連忙跑過去。我看到懸崖頂上有一個長長的黑色身影，正俯在露西的上方，那個人有一張蒼白的臉，和一雙血紅發亮的眼睛。

等我跑近些，就只有看到她一個人，她當時呼吸很不順暢。我拿披巾裹住她，用別針把披巾固定在脖子周圍，好讓她保暖。然後我才叫醒她，帶她回家。

同日，中午　露西看起來好多了。不過別針一定弄傷她了，因為我注意到她的脖子上有兩個小紅點。

P. 45

8月12日　昨夜，我被露西吵醒了兩次，她又想出門了。

8月13日　我半夜醒來，當時露西正指著一隻大蝙蝠，蝙蝠靠她靠得很近。

8月14日　今天，我們在長椅上消磨了一天。返家途中，我們停下來欣賞夕陽。這時露西突然喃喃自語說：「他的紅眼睛！簡直一模一樣。」她望向我們剛坐過的椅子，那裡坐著一個黑色的人影，那個人的眼睛像兩團大火球。

露西早早就上床。我到外面散步，思念著強納生。而當我返回時，我看到露西正探出窗戶，而她的身邊坐著一個看起來很像大鳥的東西。

我趕緊跑回臥房，但露西這時已經躺回床上，睡得很沉。她的手擱在脖子上，很疲倦的樣子，臉色也比平常蒼白。

8月17日　露西的母親告訴我，露西的心跳很微弱，可能不久於人世了。露西不知道這件事。還是沒有強納生的消息，而露西則愈來愈虛弱。

我把房間的鑰匙繫在自己的手腕上保管好。夜裡，露西來回走動，坐在打開的窗戶旁。我注意到她喉嚨上的針孔，傷口變大了。

P. 46

日記

- 米娜的日記裡寫了哪些不同的事件？
- 你認為她為什麼寫日記？
- 為什麼她的日記對她自己或我們有幫助？
- 你寫日記嗎？
- 你在日記裡寫些什麼？
- 你會重讀自己的日記，或允許別人讀你的日記嗎？

惠特比的薩繆・畢林頓父子律師事務所，給倫敦卡特帕特森公司的信函

8月17日

敬啟者：

隨函附上大北方鐵路公司所寄送的發票。該批貨物預計明日抵達國王十字車站，到站後請隨即運往普夫里附近的卡菲莊園。隨信並附上鑰匙。請將五十個箱子放置於禮拜室，即平面圖上所標示之「A」處。離開時，請將鑰匙留在大廳。

您誠摯的

薩繆・畢林頓父子敬上

P. 47

箱子

- 信中提到的箱子是誰的？
- 箱子從哪裡運來的？又準備運往何處？
- 為什麼你會認為那些箱子很重要？

米娜・墨瑞的日記

8月18日　露西好多了。我問她那一夜晚在長椅的事。

她說：「那不像是夢，感覺很真實。不知道為什麼，我當時就很想到長椅那裡。我感到害怕，隱約記得有一個黑黑的東西，它有一雙紅眼睛，就像我們那天傍晚所看到的一樣。我覺得旁邊還有一種又甜又苦的東西圍住我。」

P. 48

8月19日　開心、開心、開心！終於有強納生的消息了。親愛的他病了。霍金斯先生派人送信來給我。我今早要啟程去幫忙照顧強納生，並且把他帶回家。

布達佩斯聖約瑟夫暨聖瑪莉醫院的艾葛莎修女，寄給米娜・墨瑞小姐的信函

8月12日

親愛的女士：

我依強納生・哈克所託寫這封信，他因為身體虛弱，無法動筆。他來我們這裡已經六個星期了，他得了嚴重的腦膜炎。他希望我代為轉達他的愛意。他需要多休息，也請您前來支付他在此的花費。

您誠摯的朋友給予同情與祝福

艾葛莎修女敬上

附言：我的病人睡著了。我打開這封信多寫一些。他受到恐怖的驚嚇，胡言亂語地說著狼、血、鬼魂和惡魔的事。我之前就想寫信給您，但我們對他一無所知。他的狀況比較好了，我相信再過幾個星期就會完全康復了。

第九章

P. 49

米娜・哈克給露西・魏斯頓的信函

8月24日，布達佩斯

最親愛的露西：

我現在在布達佩斯。強納生非常蒼白、孱弱。他受了可怕的驚嚇，不記得任何事情。不過，他把日記交給我保管，他的祕密都在日記裡。他說如果我想看的話可以看，但是不需要告訴他內容，除非有重大理由。我安全地收好這本日記了。

露西，我們今天在醫院結婚了，所以強納生現在是我的丈夫。

永遠愛你的

米娜・哈克

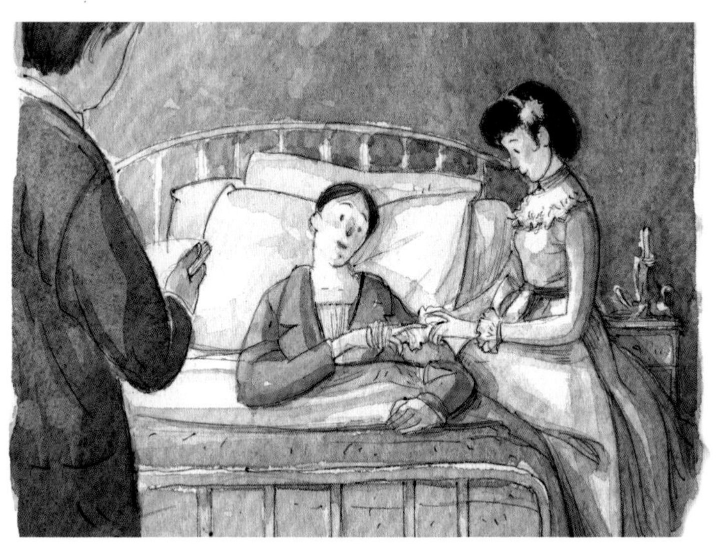

P.51

露西・魏斯頓的日記

8 月 24 日，希林漢　我應該跟米娜學學，把事情寫下來。昨晚，我又做夢了，大概是因為回到希林漢的家吧。我感到恐懼、虛弱且疲憊。

8 月 25 日　又一個折磨人的夜晚。我在午夜驚醒，因為有東西在抓搔窗戶。我做了更多的惡夢，我覺得好虛弱啊。我的臉色一定很蒼白，而且我的喉嚨很痛。母親的狀況也不好。

亞瑟・洪伍給朋友西渥醫師的信函

8 月 31 日，艾貝瑪飯店

親愛的約翰：

我需要你的幫助。露西病了，她的情況看起很不好，而且日益惡化。她已經同意要見你。請你明天來希林漢共進午餐，並為她做個檢查。我心中充滿焦慮，在你為她看過診後，我想與你單獨談談。

亞瑟

P.52

西渥醫師給亞瑟・洪伍的信函

9 月 2 日，普夫里精神病院

親愛的朋友：

很遺憾我到希林漢時，你得去探視你父親。我希望他有好轉。關於露西的病情，我找不到生理上的原因。她似乎缺血，但並沒有貧血患者常見的症狀。所以問題一定出在心理層面。她抱怨呼吸困難、嗜睡，而且惡夢連連，醒來後卻不記得夢的內容。

我已經請一位老友凡赫辛教授從阿姆斯特丹趕來，他在大學教書，對這樣的怪病懂得很多。

你永遠的朋友

約翰　西渥

P.53

西渥醫師給亞瑟・洪伍的信函

9 月 3 日，普夫里精神病院

親愛的亞瑟：

凡赫辛已經到來，並做了詳細的檢查。他說露西的病不是生理因素造成的，露西流失很多血，但並不是貧血。但凡事必事出有因，他已經回去研究了。我們每天都會拍電報給他，如果有需要，他會再回來。

你永遠的朋友

約翰・西渥

倫敦普夫里西渥醫師給阿姆斯特丹凡赫辛的電報

9 月 6 日　病情惡化，急轉直下。立刻趕來。

露西

- 露西出了什麼事？誰試圖幫助她？
- 他們知道露西怎麼了嗎？
- 你認為凡赫辛幫得了她嗎？

第十章

P. 54

西渥醫師的日記

9月7日　在希林漢，凡赫辛看到露西後，說道：「她會因缺血而死，必須立刻輸血！」

亞瑟在現場，他同意提供自己的血。露西的臉頰迅速回復了生命跡象，亞瑟卻變得愈來愈蒼白與虛弱。

後來，凡赫辛移動露西的枕頭，露西衣領上的黑色緞帶跟著移動，這時我看到頸靜脈上面有兩個小孔。那兩個小孔不大，看起來令人感到礙眼。

「我今天晚上要回阿姆斯特丹，那裡有我需要的書籍和東西。千萬別讓她離開你的視線，你整晚都不能闔上眼睛，我會盡快趕回來。」凡赫辛說。

9月9日　連續兩個晚上，我都坐著陪露西，所以今晚到希林漢時，已經十分疲倦。露西要我躺在隔壁房間的沙發上休息，然後把房門打開。我立刻沉沉入睡。

P. 56

9月10日　我感覺教授的手搭在我的肩膀上，所以驚醒過來。

「我們的病人如何？」他問。

「在我走開之前都很好。」我回答。

然而當我們走進臥室時，露西的臉色卻更蒼白了。

「我們得再開始，你要提供血液。」他說。

我們馬上開始輸血，直到她的臉頰和嘴唇恢復了一些血色，我們才停止。

「你回去休息吧，今晚由我來陪露西。我們得看好她，還有，不要讓其他人知道這件事。我有重要的理由。」教授說。

9月11日　收到了一包要給教授的大蒜花。教授將露西房間裡的窗戶都牢牢地關上，然後用力把大蒜花塗抹在窗框上。他在房門的四周也做了同樣的措施。接著，他做了大蒜花圈讓露西戴在脖子上。

在露西上床時，他把花圈放好之後，說道：「小心別把花圈弄掉，而且也不要開窗戶或開門。」

露西答應之後，我們就離開了。

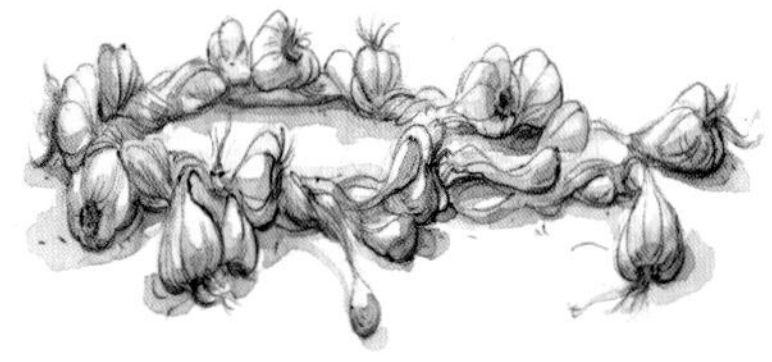

第十一章

P.57

西渥醫師的日記

9月13日　在希林漢，凡赫辛和我遇到魏斯頓夫人，她說：「昨天晚上我很擔心露西，所以就把那些味道很重的花移開，並且打開窗戶透一點新鮮空氣。」

教授的臉色霎時一陣灰白。我們進入房間時，他低語道：「果然如我所料。今天由你來操作，我來輸血。」

稍後，他告訴魏斯頓夫人，那些花是用來治病的，不可以移開。他今晚想守著露西。

露西・魏斯頓的日記

9月17日　我又慢慢恢復了體力。惡夢已遠離。窗外的拍打聲，還有會命令我去做我記不住的事的那些聲音，現在已不復見。

P.58

夜晚　今天晚上我上床時，特別留意一下那些花都有擺放好。有一隻大蝙蝠用翅膀敲擊窗戶，驚醒了我。母親走進我的房間，我請她進來陪我一起睡。窗戶的拍打聲更激烈了，接著是很大聲的玻璃碎裂聲，強風隨之灌進屋內。我看到一隻大灰狼從窗戶探頭進來。母親驚聲尖叫，她坐起來，扯掉我脖子上的花圈，然後倒地死去。

有很多黑點穿過破窗戶湧入，迴繞旋轉著。我想移動身體，卻動彈不得。

獨自跟死人一起！我也不敢出去。空氣中似乎瀰漫著黑點，隨著窗戶吹進來的風飄浮、迴轉。

第十二章

P.59

西渥醫師的日記

9月18日　凡赫辛要我昨晚去照顧露西的電報，居然遲了二十二個鐘頭！十點，我衝到希林漢，卻沒人應門。凡赫辛隨後抵達，我向他解釋整個狀況。

「我怕我們太遲了。」他說。

我們從廚房窗戶進入屋內。在露西臥室裡，她和她母親都倒臥在床上。露西臉色慘白，浮現驚恐的神情。她的喉嚨上有兩個小傷口。凡赫辛仔細聽露西的心跳，拿了一點白蘭地塗抹在她的嘴唇、牙齦、手腕和掌心。

亞瑟的朋友昆西・摩里斯此刻也抵達。正在照顧生病父親的亞瑟，請他來幫忙看看露西的情形。他馬上同意輸血救露西。

P.60

之後，我發現凡赫辛在讀露西的日記。他把日記交給我。

「裡面寫的是什麼意思？」我問。

「你以後就會懂。」他回答。

9月19日　露西每次醒來，都顯得一次比一次虛弱。我們注意到她的牙齒變得較長、較尖。下午，我們發電報給亞瑟。他抵達時，她稍微展露光采。

9月20日　昨夜，我看顧露西。窗戶和門上都是大蒜，她的脖子上也戴了花圈。我一度看到一隻盤旋的大蝙蝠，用翅膀撞擊窗戶。六點時，凡赫辛來換班，他彎下身檢查露西，當他把那些花移開後，她脖子的傷口竟消失不見了。

「她快死了，快把亞瑟叫醒！」他說。

亞瑟過來坐在她床邊，握住她的手。

她用輕柔深情的聲音說：「亞瑟，我的愛，吻我！」

凡赫辛立刻飛撲過去拉開他，說道：「為了你的性命，為了你們各自的靈魂，不要吻她！」

P. 61

露西臉上閃過憤怒的表情，露出利牙。

接著，她閉上雙眼，呼吸變得困難，最後停止。

「她死了。」凡赫辛說。

我帶亞瑟到起居室，他坐下來啜泣。接著，我回到露西房裡。

「她終於得到平靜了，一切都結束了。」我說。

「不，恐怕這才是個開始而已。」凡赫辛說。

我問他是什麼意思，他搖頭回答:「等著瞧吧！」

親吻

- 凡赫辛為什麼不讓露西親吻亞瑟？
- 她想給他哪一種親吻？如果她親吻了他，會發生什麼事？
- 你相信那種親吻會致命嗎？

第十三章

P. 63

西渥醫師的日記

翌日，我們舉行了露西的葬禮。凡赫辛在她的房間發現一些信件和日記，他將它們保留了下來。

就寢前，凡赫辛和我走進露西的房間。她躺在那裡，臉上覆蓋著白布，周圍放置了白色的花朵和蠟燭。凡赫辛輕輕掀起白布，露西的美貌讓我們兩個人都為之一嘆。凡赫辛拿來一些大蒜花，撒在露西的身體四周，並且在她嘴上放了一個小小的黃金十字架。

「明天，我會割下她的頭，挖出她的心臟。今天晚上無法進行，因為亞瑟會想看她最後一眼。等她入棺後我們再動手，這樣就不會有人知道。」他說。

「可是為什麼要這樣做？」我問。

「約翰，相信我。有一些不好的事情，你並不知道，之後還會有一些很奇怪、很恐怖的事情等著發生。」他回答。

我碰著他的手，承諾我會相信他。

P. 64

凡赫辛一早就來到我的房間。

「不用想手術的事了，太遲了。有一個僕人偷了小十字架，現在我們要繼續等下去。」他說。

後來，亞瑟抵達，他向露西告別後，屍體隨即入殮。

凡赫辛持續通宵看守露西的靈柩。

米娜・哈克的日記

9月22日，搭火車到愛塞特 今天，我們在倫敦市中心沿著皮卡迪利大道一路走著，強納生牽著我的手臂。

當我正看著一輛馬車裡坐著的一位美麗女孩時，我感覺到強納生突然緊緊抓住我的手臂。我立刻轉頭看他，發現他一臉蒼白。他驚恐地盯著一名瘦瘦高高的男人，那個男人有著一個長鼻子，留著黑色的八字鬍和山羊鬍。

那個男人也正在看著女孩，並沒有注意到我們。我仔細地打量他，他有一張冷酷無情的臉，還有大大的白牙和鮮紅的嘴唇。

那名男子

・誰是那名男子？和同伴分享你的想法。

P. 66

「你有沒有看到那個人是誰？」強納生問。

「親愛的，沒有，我不認識他。他是誰？」我說。

「那就是伯爵！但他變年輕了。」他回答。

強納生感到很痛苦。那個男人離開後，我們走到格林公園坐著。

今天的天氣頗熱，我們在陰涼處找到了一個舒適的座位。沒過幾分鐘，強納生就閉上眼睛，頭靠在我肩膀上睡著了。

等他醒來之後，他已經忘記那個陌生人的事，之後我們便搭火車回愛塞特。

晚上，凡赫辛捎來電報告知說魏斯頓夫人和露西都已經去世了。

西渥醫師的日記

9 月 22 日　露西葬在鄰近希林漢的漢普斯德。亞瑟已經和友人昆西・摩里斯回家。凡赫辛返回阿姆斯特丹，但明天會回來。他說在倫敦還有事情要處理，回來時可以來和我住。

P. 67

9 月 25 日　《西敏公報》

漢普斯德的神祕事件

近日發生幾起幼童到漢普斯德石南荒原玩耍卻晚歸的事件。幼童們表示，有一位神祕的「漂亮姐姐」邀請他們一起散步。事件發生的時間都在晚上，偶爾也有到次日清晨才被人發現的情況。所有孩童的喉嚨都有傷口，也許是老鼠或小狗造成的。警方正嚴密監管在石南荒原一帶的幼童。

漂亮姐姐

- 你想這位漂亮姐姐是誰？
- 你想這些孩童的喉嚨上為什麼會有傷口？
- 你想這位漂亮姐姐為何專挑兒童？
- 你想這則新聞會引起恐慌嗎？

第十四章

P. 68

米娜・哈克的日記

9 月 24 日　回愛塞特的家以後，我讀了強納生的日記。多麼令人毛骨悚然啊！這是真的，還是只是一種幻想？在皮卡迪利大道時，他似乎很確定就是那個黑衣男人，而且他在日記裡寫著恐怖的伯爵即將來倫敦。我開始用打字機謄寫他的日記。

凡赫辛給哈克夫人的信函

9 月 24 日

親愛的夫人：

亞瑟允許我閱讀露西的書信。既然你們是知交，我能否拜訪您討論一些事情？

凡赫辛

哈克夫人給凡赫辛的電報

9 月 25 日　今日隨時可前來。米娜・哈克

P. 69

米娜・哈克的日記

9 月 25 日　在凡赫辛抵達之前，我坐在打字機前謄寫我的日記。如果他問起露西的事，我就可以讓他看。

他讀了日記說：「米娜女士，這為我開啟了一扇門！」接著他問起了強納生的事。

「他差不多要康復了，但在倫敦時，有一個人讓他憶起那些讓他得到腦膜炎的恐怖事情。」我說。

「我今晚會留在愛塞特，我要把每件事都好好釐清一下。現在，告訴我你丈夫的困擾。」他說。

之後，我把強納生日記的打字稿拿給他，並且安排明天早上再見面。

凡赫辛給哈克夫人的信函

9 月 25 日，6 點

> 親愛的米娜夫人：
>
> 我一回到飯店就詳讀您丈夫的日記。你可以毫無疑惑地入睡。這些事情固然怪誕駭人，卻是千真萬確的！明天早上見到他時，我會有很多問題要請教他。
>
> 您最忠誠的朋友
>
> 亞伯拉罕・凡赫辛

P. 70

強納生・哈克的日記

9 月 26 日　我知道凡赫辛要來訪，而且他相信我所說的伯爵的事情。現在我知道我不害怕了，甚至不怕伯爵了！他人在倫敦，我看到的就是他。凡赫辛會把他揪出來。

我們見面時，凡赫辛說：「我眼前有個重大任務，需要一些資料，請把你遇到的每一件事情都告訴我吧。」

今天早上，我帶他到車站，買報紙給他。他突然注意到《西敏公報》上的內容，臉色霎時蒼白。

他專注地讀著報紙，喃喃自語道：「老天！這麼快！」

凡赫辛

- 凡赫辛的任務是什麼？
- 他在《西敏公報》上讀到什麼？

P. 71

西渥醫師的日記

9 月 26 日　凡赫辛於今天早晨返回倫敦。

「你有什麼看法？」他遞給我《西敏公報》後問道。

我看到報導寫道，有孩童被帶走，等被發現時喉嚨上都有小傷口。

「就像可憐的露西。」我說。

「你還不清楚露西的死因嗎？什麼造成失血的？」他問。

我搖搖頭。他繼續說：「那些幼童喉嚨上的小洞，跟露西小姐喉嚨上的洞都是同一種東西造成的嗎？」

我點點頭。

「你錯了。我希望你說的是對的，但情況很慘。那是露西小姐咬的！」

第十五章

P. 72

西渥醫師的日記（續）

「你瘋了嗎？」我大叫。

「我希望我是瘋了，這令人難以置信，但今晚，我會證明給你看。」他回答。

後來，晚上時，我們進入漢普斯德墓園。到達魏斯頓家族的墓室後，凡赫辛撬開露西的棺木蓋子，棺木裡面居然是空的！

接著我們走到外面尋找露西。那是一個寒冷、漫長的等待過程。但這時，我突然看到一道白影閃過。教授匆忙跟過去，我也跟上。模糊的白色身影朝魏斯頓墓室的方向移動。等我趕到教授身旁時，我發現他手裡抱著一名幼童。

「你現在滿意了嗎？」他說。

我點燃火柴，看著孩子的喉嚨。沒有任何記號。

「我們剛好趕上。」教授感激地說。

P. 74

9 月 27 日 午後兩點，凡赫辛再度打開棺木，而露西就躺在裡面。她真美，她的嘴唇更加紅潤，臉頰也泛著紅暈。

他拉起她的嘴唇。「你看，那些兒童讓她的牙齒現在變得更尖銳了。約翰，你現在相信了吧？她已經死了一個星期，大部分的屍體應該不會這樣。她成了活死人。我要割下她的頭，在她的嘴裡塞大蒜，再用木樁刺穿她的身體。」他說。

凡赫辛沒有立即進行這項可怕的任務，因為他想先讓亞瑟知道來龍去脈，以免他會覺得我們接下來的行動很不道德。

我們敲訂了明天晚上在他的飯店和亞瑟、昆西・摩里斯碰面。

凡赫辛在柏克萊飯店留的字條，
給約翰・西渥醫師

9 月 27 日

親愛的約翰：

我回到墓園，不希望活死人露西小姐今晚跑出去。我會用大蒜和十字架封死墓園的門，以防她出去。不過「另一個活死人」有能力找到她的墳墓。他很狡猾，他騙過我們取走了露西小姐的性命，把我們玩弄於股掌之上。如果他今晚來墓園，他就會發現我。所以我先寫下這張紙條，以防萬一。

隨信附上的文件和哈克的日記等等的東西，也請仔 細閱讀，這樣我們就能找到那個活死人頭目，割下他的頭，然後把他的心臟燒掉或是用木樁刺穿，如此一來，世界才能免於他的威脅。

凡赫辛

活死人

- 凡赫辛所說的「另一個活死人」是指誰？他是如何形容他的？
- 他們打算怎麼對付這個活死人頭目？為什麼？

第十六章

P. 76

西渥醫師的日記（續）

9 月 29 日　昨夜，亞瑟、昆西和我在凡赫辛於柏克萊飯店的房間見面。我們討論著各種計畫，但亞瑟無法接受，於是我們決定走一趟露西的墓穴。

午夜時分，凡赫辛點亮一盞燈，大家都圍著露西的棺木。

「約翰，露西小姐的屍體在昨天時是不是還在棺木裡頭？」他問。

「是的。」我回答。

但我們打開棺木之後，裡面空無一物。

接著，他在墓室四周放了聖餅。

「這樣活死人就進不來。」他解釋說。

我們走到外面躲起來。不久教授指著一個白色的身影。在月光下，我們看到一個金髮女子正俯看著一個金髮孩童。孩童尖聲哭泣。當她朝我們這邊走過來時，我們看到甜美的露西此刻變得很殘酷，而且一向純潔的她也變得很放縱。

P. 77

凡赫辛站出來，向我們做了手勢，要我們跟他一道走。我們在墓室門前站成一排，他舉起燈籠，我們看到她的嘴裡滴下鮮血，不禁嚇得打哆嗦。

她繼續往前走，兩眼發出火光，然後把孩童扔下，孩童躺在地上呻吟著。她朝亞瑟走去，張開雙臂，說：「來我這裡，亞瑟，我的雙臂多麼想擁抱你。來，親愛的，我們可以一起安眠！」

她的聲音甜美得令人難以抗拒，亞瑟恍神似地張開雙臂，凡赫辛這時拿著金色十字架，跳到他們兩人中間。

她趕緊後退，臉上露出憤怒的表情，從他身旁衝過去。

這時凡赫辛說：「亞瑟，我應該繼續嗎？」

「當然，沒有比這更恐怖的事情了。」

凡赫辛把聖餅拿開，露西便回到了棺木裡。然後，他再把聖餅放回去。

「明天才能再繼續。我們兩點來這裡。」他說。

9 月 29 日　今天，打開棺木時，我們看到露西躺在裡面。

「這真的是露西的身體嗎？」亞瑟問。

「你可以說是，也可以說不是。不過很快你會看到她原來的樣子，或是說看到她現在的樣子。」凡赫辛回答。

P. 78

他從袋子裡取出裝備，包括一根一公尺長、有一頭削得很尖的圓木樁。他說：「在我們開始之前，我先跟你們說明一下。人在變成活死人之後，就成了不死之身。他們會一直活下去，然後就會不斷有新的受害者，因為被活死人咬死的人，也會變成活死人。這位不幸小姐的人生才剛要開始，那些被她吸過血的孩童還不算危險，不過如果她繼續活下去，孩童也會跟著產生變化。而如果她死了，孩童會恢復正常。當這個活死人一旦變成真正的死人，那麼露西的靈魂也會獲得自由。因此，準備將木樁敲下去的手，是一隻受到祝福的手，能夠讓她得到自由。」

大家都看著亞瑟。他向前跨一步說：「跟我說應該要怎麼做，我可以做到。」

凡赫辛給亞瑟木樁和榔頭，告訴他用榔頭把木樁敲穿過她的心臟。

亞瑟在執行時，凡赫辛為死者唸誦了特殊的祈禱文。

棺木裡的『那個東西』放聲尖叫、全身顫抖扭曲，鮮血從心臟流出，但亞瑟沒有住手，露西的身體最後終於靜止不動。

我們看著棺木，看到了熟悉的露西，有著一張甜美與純潔的臉龐。

P. 80

亞瑟轉向凡赫辛說：「謝謝你！你讓親愛的露西重獲靈魂，而且給了我平靜。」

我們先讓亞瑟和昆西離開墓室，然後鋸斷木樁上方，將樁尖留在她體內。接著，我們割下她的頭，在她嘴裡塞進大蒜。最後我們蓋緊棺木，收拾好工具，離開墓室。教授鎖上門，並且把鑰匙交給亞瑟。

「現在，我的朋友，我們第一步的工作已經完成，接下來還有更重大的任務：找出這一切悲劇的始作俑者，然後消滅他。這將是漫長而艱難的任務，而且會有危險與痛苦。你們要協助我嗎？」

我們一一握住他的手，允諾會幫忙。

「我們後天晚上碰面，一起用餐，到時候會有另外兩個你們不認識的人也會來參與，然後我會跟大家說明計畫。」教授解釋說。

第二步

- 他們的任務完成了哪一步？第二步的任務是什麼？
- 你覺得第二步會比第一步困難嗎？
- 你知道另外兩個人是誰嗎？猜猜看。

第十七章

P. 81

西渥醫師的日記（續）

我們抵達飯店時，凡赫辛接到一通電報：

「正搭火車前來。強納生在惠特比。有重大的消息。米娜」

我去接哈克夫人，帶她回我家。晚上，我再次詳讀她丈夫的日記，她則用打字機謄錄我的日記。

9月30日　哈克先生和他的妻子花了一整天時間，把所有的日記、信件和其他文件等等，按時間順序排列出來，以便可以更清楚地呈現出整個事件。一想到我住的這間療養院隔壁的卡菲莊園，有可能就是伯爵的藏身處，感覺就怪怪的！

P. 82

強納生・哈克的日記

9月29日　在惠特比和畢林頓先生碰面，追查伯爵的貨物。我看到「五十箱一般土壤」的發票，還有伯爵的信件和指示，也拿到寄給倫敦的卡特・帕特森的信件和回函副本。

9月30日　我在國王十字車站和火車站長碰面，查到了記錄：箱子的數量相同。接著，我到卡特・帕特森的辦公室調閱文件。現在，我知道由迪麥特號運送，從瓦爾納出發，抵達惠特比的五十個箱子，全部都搬進了卡菲莊園的禮拜室。

第十八章

P. 83

西渥醫師的日記

9月30日　亞瑟和昆西抵達，詳讀我們的文件。後來，我去接凡赫辛。晚餐後，我給了他一份所有資料的副本。

米娜・哈克的日記

9月30日　我們在西渥醫師的書房集合。教授說：「我們都看過資料了，的確有吸血鬼這種生物。混入人群中的這個吸血鬼，他力量強大，而且很狡猾。

他可以在某個範圍內，以各種化身隨心所欲地出現。他也可以在一定的範圍內，操縱暴風雨、濃霧、雷電，並且控制老鼠、蝙蝠、貓頭鷹和狼等動物。他能夠改變身形的大小，隨意地消失和出現。我們正在進行的是一項很恐怖的任務，各位要和我並肩作戰嗎？」

我們站起來，握住彼此的手，圍成一圈，都同意加入。

凡赫辛繼續說：「吸血鬼需要活人的血，這可以讓他們變年輕。他們不吃東西，沒有影子或倒影，而且很強壯。

P. 85

我們遇到的這個吸血鬼能變成狼或蝙蝠，可以在他所製造的霧氣中現身，像沙塵那樣隨月光飛來。他可以進出任何地方。不過，他也有極限，他不能進入未經邀請的地方。白天時，他的力量會停止，他要睡在裝有土壤的箱子中，而那些土壤是從他的城堡運來的。有些物品可以移除他的力量：在他棺木上放進大蒜、十字架或玫瑰花枝，可以阻止他出來。木樁和割下頭顱才能讓他安息，就像我們看到的露西那樣。因此，再找到他的藏身之處後，我們要把他困在棺木裡，再殺了他。現在，我們要到隔壁看看那五十個箱子是否還在，如果不在，就要把每一個箱子都找出來。最後，米娜女士，你的工作現在就告一段落。您太珍貴了，不能冒這個險。」

第十九章

P. 86

強納生・哈克的日記

10 月 1 日，凌晨 5 點　我們拿到了一個十字架、大蒜花圈、一把左輪手槍、一把刀子、一個電燈，還有一個裝著聖餅的信封。

西渥用萬能鑰匙打開卡菲莊園的門。

凡赫辛從大廳的桌子上拿起鑰匙，說：「強納生，你描繪過這裡的平面圖，所以帶我們去禮拜室吧。」

教授打開橡木製的小門，裡頭傳出一股混著滯悶的空氣、鮮血和泥土的惡臭味。

「數一數箱子的數量。」凡赫辛說。

只有二十九個！我們在尋找箱子同

時，我看到昆西突然從一個角落往後退，我們看到一大片磷光，像星星般閃閃發亮。接著，整個地方竄滿了老鼠。似乎已有所準備的亞瑟衝到門邊，把門打開。他拿出銀哨子，然後吹響哨子，隨後便跑進來了三隻狗。等狗一進來，所有的老鼠馬上消失。

我們搜遍整個房子，找到了從渥華茲來的運送工人約瑟夫・史莫里先生所留下的收據。

P. 87

黎明到來，我們離開。凡赫辛從一大串鑰匙中拿出前門鑰匙，然後鎖上門，將那把鑰匙保管起來。

等我回到我們的房間時，我發現米娜正在熟睡中，她的臉色看起來比平常蒼白。

米娜・哈克的日記

10 月 1 日　昨晚，男士們離開後，我沒有睡意。我望向窗外，看到一縷白色薄霧越過草地飄過來。

我上了床，後來又起身看看窗外。霧氣變濃了，往房子壓過來，彷彿要爬上窗戶一般。

我做了一個奇怪的夢，我夢到自己全身動彈不得，霧氣瀰漫整個房間，所有東西都被重重的冷空氣給籠罩住。這時霧氣變成了柱狀，牆上瓦斯燈的紅光也變成了兩隻紅色的眼睛。

我記得的最後一幕，是有一張死白的臉正俯看著我。

第二十章

P. 89

強納生・哈克的日記

10 月 1 日，晚上　到渥華茲拜訪約瑟夫・史莫里。

他記得去了卡菲莊園，搬走那些失蹤的箱子。他說有六個箱子送到麥恩鎮契克森巷 197 號，另外六個送到伯蒙西的牙買加巷。他正打聽其他箱子的去處。

米娜很快就入睡，臉色很蒼白。我想她很擔心。

10 月 2 日，晚上　今天早上，史莫里告訴我有位布洛克森先生，運送了九個箱子到皮卡迪利大道的一個地址；他描述了那間房子的外觀。我去皮卡迪利

大道後，很快就認出那個房子。在進一步探查後，最後我找出皮卡迪利大道 347 號的屋主，是一個叫作德維爾伯爵的外國貴族。

箱子

- 你想箱子為什麼會分散送到不同的房子？
- 德維爾伯爵是誰？

第二十一章

P. 90

西渥醫師的日記

10 月 3 日　昨晚，有一位住在療養院的精神病患發生意外，他叫做藍菲爾。藍菲爾的頭骨破裂，背脊摔斷。凡赫辛趕來後，我們降低藍菲爾的腦壓，希望他能開口說話。亞瑟和昆西加入我們。

藍菲爾睜開眼睛說：「我做了一個惡夢。」

接著，凡赫辛用很嚴肅的口氣小聲說：「藍菲爾先生，告訴我們你的夢境。」

「不，那不是夢，」藍菲爾說：「那是一個恐怖的真實事件。」他停了一下，然後繼續說道：「他像平常一樣，從霧氣中爬到窗口。第一次他有形體，他眼神發亮、充滿憤怒。他大笑著，嘴唇很紅，有一口尖利的白牙。接著，他允諾我一些事情，所以我請他進來，他便從窗縫中溜進來。不過他今天晚上沒有陪我，而是去追逐其他人。我很生氣，因為我希望他能陪我。我緊抓住那團霧，但他可怕的眼神好像要把我燒掉一樣，所以我就放開手。他把我整個人舉起來摔下，然後那團霧就從門下面的縫隙溜走了。」

P. 91

「我們現在知道最壞的情況發生了，不過也許還不算太遲。我們去警告哈克夫婦！我們的所有傢伙都要帶上，現在刻不容緩了！」凡赫辛說。

凡赫辛轉動哈克夫婦房門的門把，但門打不開，於是我們一夥人便朝門撞上去，房門應聲被撞開。

明亮的月光透過窗戶照進來，照亮了我們眼前的恐怖景象。

強納生躺在床上，一身白衣的米娜跪在床邊，而一個黑色的身影就站在她旁邊。那是伯爵，他正掐住米娜的臉，用手抓著她往他的胸前靠近，強迫她喝下鮮血。米娜的白色睡袍血跡斑斑。

我們衝進房間時，伯爵的眼睛彷彿燃燒紅色火焰，他尖銳的白牙，像野獸一樣張牙舞爪。他把米娜往後甩，朝我們撲過來。

凡赫辛拿起裝有聖餅的信封，伯爵停下腳步往退後。我們大家都舉起十字架，朝他逼近。

這時，一片烏雲遮住了月亮，而當昆西打開瓦斯燈時，我們看到一縷輕煙從門底下鑽走。

P. 93

霧氣

- 那團霧氣是什麼？
- 列出德古拉在故事中出現的方式。

亞瑟和昆西跑出去找他。

等亞瑟回來時，說道：「到處都找不到他，他把手稿和留聲機記錄都銷毀了。」

「謝天謝地，還有另一份副本放在保險箱！」我打岔。

「樓下沒有他的蹤影，所以我就去藍菲爾的房間找。那可憐的傢伙死了。昆西，你呢？」亞瑟繼續說道。

「我在外面時，看到了一隻蝙蝠從藍菲爾的窗戶飛出來。我以為會看到他飛進卡菲莊園，但顯然他是去了其他的藏身之處。東方的天空已經出現紅光了。」

凡赫辛對米娜說話。

P. 94

「伯爵進來我的房間，如果我不安靜，他就要殺了強納生。然後，他吸了我的血，我無法抵抗他。接著，他很生氣我跟你們大家站在同一陣線。他為了要懲罰我，就強迫我喝下他的血，所以他在自己的胸口劃了一個傷口。」她說。

米娜

- 米娜發生了什麼事？
- 她現在很危險，有可能變成什麼？
- 你認為其他人能解救她嗎？

第二十二章

P.95

強納生・哈克的日記

10月3日　我們六點半開會。凡赫辛有個計畫，希望我們找出伯爵所有的箱子，然後再用聖餅來淨化消毒，這樣伯爵就無法使用這些箱子了。

離開前，凡赫辛在米娜的房間裡放置了一些東西，以防止德古拉進來。接著，他用聖餅碰觸她額頭，保護她不受伯爵影響。然而，聖餅一碰到她的皮膚就立刻燙傷了她，讓她發出了恐怖的尖叫聲。

我留下沉重的心情。首先，我們到卡菲莊園，淨化那裡的箱子。接下來，我們決定到皮卡迪利大道的房子。我們搭火車到倫敦市中心，找了鎖匠協助我們進屋。屋子裡面有一股惡臭。我們在餐廳裡找到了八個箱子，於是在每個箱子裡各放一塊聖餅進去。

不過，還有一個箱子不見了，為了完成任務，我們一定要找到箱子。屋子裡頭的其他地方都空無一物。有一個桌上放了皮卡迪利大道、伯蒙西和麥恩鎮房子的文件，還有幾把鑰匙。亞瑟和昆西拿走那些鑰匙，要去淨化放在伯蒙西和麥恩鎮的箱子。兩位醫生和我等待他們回來——或是等待伯爵到來。

第二十三章

P.96

西渥醫師的日記

10月3日　送電報的男孩帶來消息：「12:45，小心『德』。他現在離開卡菲莊園，往南走。米娜。」

沒多久，亞瑟和昆亞回來了，他們已經把其他的箱子也淨化了。

「他很快就會來這裡，你們要把傢伙都準備好。」凡赫辛說。

當我們聽到鑰匙在門鎖裡轉動時，大夥人都已經就定位了。但伯爵早有準備，他跳進房間，在我們還來不及行動之前就掠過了我們。哈克擋住另一道門，用長刀刺向他的心臟，可是伯爵的速度太快，刀子只劃破了他的大衣，鈔

票和金幣散落一地。

我握住十字架和聖餅往前移動，接著看到這個怪物往退後。其他人也跟著做同樣的動作，哈克拿刀往伯爵刺過去，但伯爵從刀下鑽了過去，然後從地板上抓起一些錢，迅速地奔向房間的另一頭，最後跳下窗戶。

P.97

我們追過去，看到他爬上階梯，穿越庭院。他推開馬廄的門，轉身說：「你們以為你們贏得了我！你們會後悔的！你們以為我沒有地方躲，但是我有。你們的女孩已經成為我的人了，不久，你們也會變成我的人。」

他進入馬廄，鎖上身後的門。

我們往門廳移動時，教授說：「他怕我們，也怕時間。他為什麼要這麼匆忙？為什麼拿錢？快追上他。我留下來，以免他回來拿東西。」

教授把剩下的錢和房屋地契放入口袋。亞瑟和昆西很快返回，沒有發現德古拉的蹤跡。此時接近日落時分，因此我們懷著沉重的心情回到我家，哈克夫人正等著我們。晚餐過後，教授布置哈克的房間，以防吸血鬼來犯。

強納生・哈克的日記

10 月 4 日，清晨　米娜叫醒我說：「你快去找教授，讓他趁天亮前把我催眠，我覺得到時候可以盡情地把事情說出來了。」

教授抵達後，用他的手在她頭的四周圍快速移動。米娜被催眠後，他問：「你現在在哪裡？」

P.98

「這裡一片漆黑，我聽到外面有水流聲。」她說。

「你在船上嗎？」他問。

「是的！我聽得到頭頂上有腳步聲和鐵鍊的咯吱聲。」

「你在做什麼？」

「我一動也不動，就像死了，」米娜回答。

在太陽升起時，她閉上了眼睛。

「現在我們知道伯爵在想什麼了。他想逃跑，我們要追上他。不過我們先休息一下。我們很安全，因為我們和他之間隔著河水，他無法過河。」教授說。

「我們為什麼要窮追不捨？他已經離開了啊。」米娜問。

「親愛的米娜女士，因為他可以活好幾百年，而你是肉身凡夫。現在，時間很重要，因為你的喉嚨上有他的印記。」凡赫辛說。

第二十四章

P.99

米娜・哈克的日記

10 月 5 日，下午 5 點　狀況是：伯爵正搭船返回川夕凡尼亞。昨天到今天之間，開往黑海的唯一船隻就是「凱薩琳沙皇號」。伯爵和他的箱子已經登船，正在前往瓦爾納的路上。

西渥醫師的日記

10 月 5 日　凡赫辛說：「米娜女士

正在起變化，我們要有所準備。她的臉上開始出現吸血鬼的特徵——牙齒較尖銳、眼神較凶狠。我擔心伯爵能讀她的心思。」

我點頭同意。

「我們不要跟她講我們計畫，以免她跟伯爵透露。」他繼續說道。

第二十五章

P. 100

西渥醫師的日記

10 月 11 日　昨天日落時，米娜說：「我知道自己要變成露西那個樣子了。請答應我，你們會用木樁刺穿我，並且割下我的頭顱。」

我們都牽起她的手，承諾會這樣做。

然後她繼續說：「那個時刻可能會很快而且無預警地就到來，到時候你們一定要立刻動手，不然我就會變成你們的敵人。」

10 月 28 日　我們在十二日離開英國，搭火車橫跨大陸，十五日抵達瓦爾納，等待凱薩琳沙皇號入港。但是我們今天接到電報說，那艘船正要進入多瑙河的加拉茲港。

凡赫辛擔心伯爵讀了米娜的心思，知道我們正在瓦爾納，所以改變旅程以逃離我們。

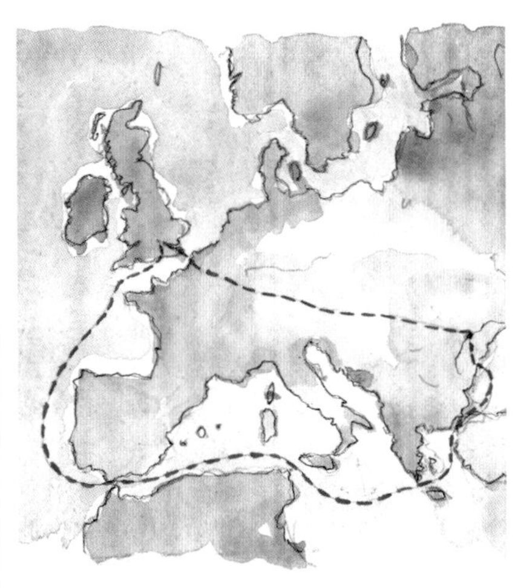

第二十六章

P. 102

強納生・哈克的日記

10月30日　我們登上凱薩琳沙皇號，發現箱子已經轉交給一個叫作史金斯基的男子。不過，就在我們談話之際，有人跑來通報說史金斯基死了。他的喉嚨被撕裂，看起來像是遭到了野獸的攻擊！

米娜研究了地圖，她認為箱子是經由水路運送過去的，船隻進入畢斯崔扎河的匯流處，繞過波戈隘口，那裡是最接近德古拉城堡的地方。

我們決定，由我和亞瑟搭乘蒸汽快艇，而昆西和西渥則騎馬沿河岸前進。在這期間，凡赫辛和米娜搭會火車到維爾斯地，然後再搭馬車到德古拉的城堡。

第二十七章

P. 104

亞伯拉罕・凡赫辛的備忘錄

11月4日　給倫敦普夫里的約翰・西渥，以防我再也見不到他。

我在營火旁邊這則備忘錄。天氣極冷，很快就會下雪。米娜夫人一直在睡覺。我們昨天在日出後抵達波戈隘口。我為米娜催眠，她說：「一片漆黑，水流動聲。」

我們開始沿小路走。日落時分，我無法催眠米娜夫人。我升火，她為我煮了些食物，但她自己並不餓。她睜著明亮的雙眼望著我。她在睡夢中看起來逐漸恢復健康，這讓我感到害怕。

11月5日，早晨　昨天，我們在城堡下方紮營。我在雪中繞著米娜夫人畫一個圈，然後把捏碎的聖餅撒在圓圈上。

「到這裡來。」我說道，以便測試。

她走了一步後停止，說：「我不行。」

P. 106

之後開始下雪，我看到三個女人的形體在霧氣中迴旋。我想多加一些柴火，但米娜女士說：「待在圓圈裡，在這裡很安全。」

迴旋的身影向她靠近，但始終無法進入圓圈裡。接著，她們化成強納生在城堡裡看到的那三名女子。她們指著米娜女士。

「來吧，姐妹，到我們這邊來！」她們用甜膩的嗓音說。

米娜女士的眼中充滿恐懼。我感到高

興，因為那表示她還未成為她們其中的一員。

西渥的日記

11 月 5 日　黎明時分，我們看到一些吉普賽人駕著大型貨車從河邊離開。雪花輕飄，狼群嚎叫。

凡赫辛醫師的備忘錄

11 月 5 日，下午　我把米娜女士留在聖圈裡，獨自前往城堡。我很快就在那裡找到老舊的禮拜室，並且看到那三名女吸血鬼正躺著睡覺。她們長得很漂亮，讓我差一點要手軟了。我延遲行動，忍不住地一直凝視著她們。但我隨即想到米娜女士，於是振作精神執行任務。

P. 107

我一一查過禮拜室裡的所有墳墓，發現只有這三個活死人幽靈。另外有一個較大的墳墓，上面只寫著一個名字：

德古拉

這就是吸血鬼王的活死人之家。我放了一些聖餅進去，讓他永遠回不來。接著，我開始進行恐怖任務。當木樁刺進她們的身體，她們發出的淒厲尖叫和痛苦扭曲的形體極為嚇人。然而，我在每個人的臉上都看到喜悅，因為她們的靈魂終於獲勝。我用刀割下每個人的頭顱後，她們整個身體就化為塵土。

當我踏進米娜女士睡覺的圓圈時，她醒起來說：「我們去找我的丈夫，他正朝這邊趕來。」

P. 108

米娜・哈克的日記

11 月 6 日　教授和我開始朝著我知道強納生會來的方向前進。我們聽到遠處傳來的狼嚎聲。

我感到疲倦，教授在一塊巨石下找到一個遮風避雨的地方，幫我鋪了毛皮床。接著他拿出望遠鏡，開始在地平線視察。

突然，他大喊：「你看！米娜女士！你看！」

我看到吉普賽人騎馬拉著一個大型貨車，貨車上擺放著一個方形大箱子。這一幕讓我感到害怕。當我正看著時，教授在我們的腳下畫出一個大圓圈，並捏碎一些聖餅撒在周圍。

「至少你在這裡很安全，不會受到他的威脅！」他說道，然後繼續用望遠鏡偵察。

「他們移動的速度很快，要趕在日落前抵達。」然後他又大喊：「你看！昆西和西渥正從南邊趕過來！」

我接過望遠鏡看到兩個人，之後我看到強納生和亞瑟從北方快速趕過來。我跟教授通報，他開心地大叫：「他們都會合了，我們會包圍住吉普賽人。」

他拿出步槍，我也拿出手槍。透過望遠鏡，我看到狼群從四面八方聚集而來。

P.110

終場

- 列出這個場景中所有不同的人物、動物和目標。為什麼他們都會合在一起了？
- 你覺得這個結尾令人興奮嗎？

吉普賽人和我們的友人愈來愈靠近。教授和我備好槍等待著。

突然強納生和昆西大叫：「停！」

吉普賽領袖下令同伴繼續前進，但有四個男人舉起來福槍，命令他們停止。

吉普賽人迅速圍住貨車，對我們亮出他們的刀槍。

強納生和昆西下定決心要在日落前完成任務。強納生跳上貨車，用大刀開始撬開箱子的蓋子。昆西也上前幫忙撬另一邊，一隻手捂住腹部的傷口。蓋子隨即被撬開。

吉普賽人最後放棄了。太陽這時即將落入峰頂後方，當他們看到西沉的落日時，露出了勝利的眼神，這時伯爵躺在裝有泥土的箱子裡，紅色的眼睛怒目而視。

P.111

日落時分

- 為什麼在日落前殺死伯爵如此重要？

接著，強納生的大刀一閃，劃過伯爵的喉嚨，昆西的刀也同時刺入他的心臟。德古拉的全身以不可思議的速度，粉碎化為塵埃。在那一刻，伯爵的臉上閃過平靜的神情。

吉普賽人嚇得一句話也説不出來，轉身駕車逃走，狼群也隨之而去。

這一瞬間，昆西・摩里斯倒地，鮮血仍從指間流出。我跑到他的身旁，兩位醫生也是。他拉著我的手，對我微笑。

「我很高興可以為你服務，我死而無憾。」他説。

就這樣，他走了，留給我們苦澀的悲傷。

後記

P. 112

七年前，我們都到地獄走過一趟，但我們覺得，我們當中有些人自此以後所擁有的幸福，讓當時候的那一場苦難變得很值得。讓我和米娜更開心的是，我們的兒子昆西出生那一天，正好是昆西・摩里斯的忌日。

今年夏天，我們重遊川夕凡尼亞，去了一些充滿恐怖回憶的地方。我們難以置信當時候所見到、所聽到的那一切，竟然都是真的，而城堡依然矗立在荒蕪的山林之上。

亞瑟和西渥後來也各自成婚，幸福美滿。我從保險箱取出放了好幾年的文件，當中除了後來寫的筆記和凡赫辛的備忘錄，其他的大量文件都是打字稿，我知道，這些無法當成有效文件來證實事件。

凡赫辛總結説：「我們不需要證明，不要求任何人相信。你們的小孩昆西有一天會知道，他的母親是一位多麼勇敢

的女性。他已經深知她的溫柔與慈愛，以後有一天他也會了解，有些男子是如何地愛著她。為了她，他們不惜冒險犯難。」

強納生・哈克

ANSWER KEY

Before Reading

Page 9

3 c
4 b, c

Page 11

7 a) 5 b) 4 c) 6 d) 1 e) 3 f) 2

Page 12

8
a) b b) d c) f d) e e) a f) c

9
a) 6 b) 8 c) 5 d) 3
e) 4 f) 2 g) 1 h) 7

Page 13

10
a) earth b) lizard c) coffin
d) pin e) bench f) razor
g) throat h) cart

Page 20
- A carriage and horses appears. The wolves howl.

Page 30
- There was a child in a bag. The women were given the bag and they passed through the window with it, obviously intending to eat it.

Page 34
- Prisoner.
- The wolves.

Page 35
- To feed on people's blood.

Page 39
- Her friend Lucy.

Page 46
- Letters, her own notes and newspaper articles.
- The diary is useful because it helps both her and us to keep track of events.

Page 47
- Count Dracula's.
- From Transylvania and Whitby.
- To Carfax in Purfleet.

Page 53
- She has lost a lot of blood.
- Arthur, Dr Seward and Professor Van Helsing.
- Not yet.

Page 61
- Because she will contaminate him.
- She wants to take his blood. He could become a vampire, too.

Page 67
- Lucy.
- Because she has taken their blood.

Page 70

- To find and stop Count Dracula.
- About another incident related to Count Dracula

Page 75

- Count Dracula. Cunning.
- Cut off his head and burn or drive a stake through his heart. To kill him.

Page 80

- They have "released" Lucy's soul.
- To do the same to Count Dracula.
- Two other people are Jonathan and Mina Harker.

Page 89

- So he has different places to "sleep."
- Count Dracula.

Page 93

- Count Dracula.

Page 94

- She has been "bitten" by Count Dracula.
- A vampire.

Page 110

- Wolves, Mina, Van Helsing, gypsies, horses, cart, square box (Count Dracula), binoculars, Jonathan, Arthur, Quincey, Seward, Winchester, pistol.
- To put Count Dracula to "rest."

Page 111

- Because he will "wake up" and become strong again.

After Reading

Page 116

9

a) F b) T c) T d) F
e) F f) T g) F

10 a) 5 b) 3 c) 1 d) 6 e) 4 f) 2

Page 117

11

a) Vampires can appear when and where they want in various forms. They can to some extent control storms, fog and thunder and creatures such as rats, bats, owls, and wolves. They can change size, vanish and reappear. They do not eat, or make shadows or reflections, and they are extremely strong.
b) Vampires need the blood of the living, which makes them grow younger. They may not enter any place until they are invited. Their power stops with daylight and they must sleep in the boxes of earth. Some things remove their power: garlic, the crucifix or a rose branch on the coffin all stops their power.
c) A vampire can be defeated by a stake through the heart and the head cut off.

12

Five: Lucy, three vampire women, Count Dracula.

13

a) When he appeared to Lucy in Whitby and when he came to take her blood. In Carfax after Renfield died.
b) When he appeared to Renfield at Carfax. When he appeared to Mina in her room in Carfax for the first time. When he left Mina and Jonathan in their bedroom to escape from the others.
c) Jumping off the *Demeter* in Whitby.

14 In the chapel at Count Dracula's house in Carfax.

15

a) They appear to Jonathan Harker when he is in the Count's castle and falls asleep in a moonlit room.
b) Two were dark, and reminded Jonathan of the Count, and the other had wavy, golden hair and blue eyes. Each one had white shiny teeth and red lips.
c) Because he has forbidden them to touch Jonathan.
d) Van Helsing drives stakes through their hearts and puts them to rest.

Page 118

16

a) Mr Hawkins. He is Jonathan's employer. He merely sends Jonathan to the Count.
b) Quincey Morris. He helps Lucy when Arthur is unable to come, and he gives her some of his blood. He helps to catch the Count and in the end he dies. He is shot in the stomach.
c) Renfield. The Count uses him to get to Mina Harker. In the end Renfield dies.
d) Samuel F. Billington. He merely sends the boxes as directed by the Count.

Page 119

19

a) Count Dracula, to Jonathan Harker, in the castle to stop coming to harm.
b) Lucy, to Mina, on their bench in Whitby talking about the Count.
c) Van Helsing, to Dr Seward, talking about Lucy.
d) Van Helsing, to Dr Seward, talking about Lucy.
e) Count Dracula, to Van Helsing, etc., in London, talking about his victims.
f) Mina, to Van Helsing, etc. talking about becoming a vampire.

Page 120

20 (possible answers)
a) She tries to warn Harker.
b) They supposedly burn where treasure is hidden.

c) He needs to help the Count buy a house in England.
d) It is huge and dark on a steep mountain.
e) They are frightening but attractive.
f) Lots of them were filled and taken away. Later they were sent to England.
g) It was shipwrecked at Whitby and it brought the Count to England.
h) They are great friends.
i) She is anxious and an easy victim for the Count.
j) They are pinpricks or marks from the Count's teeth.
k) They are things that keep vampires away.
l) They are Lucy's victims.
m) Van Helsing and Dr Seward see Lucy at work as a vampire.
n) They are places for the Count to rest.
o) They are things that keep vampires away.
p) It takes place across land and sea.
q) He comes to a dramatic but just end.

Page 121

23

a) Letters, journals, diaries and articles.
b) Jonathan Harker, with the help of his wife.
c) Four: Jonathan Harker, Mina Harker, Lucy, Dr Seward.

Page 122

26

a) on b) at c) in front of d) to
e) over f) into g) beside h) in

28

a) into b) in front of
c) up, along d) with

Page 123

30 (possible answers)

a) Where will Dracula's carriage meet Jonathan Harker? It will meet him at the Borgo Pass.
b) How long will Jonathan stay at the Count's castle? He will stay as long as the Count wants.
c) Why will Lucy die? She will die because the Count takes her blood.
d) How will Van Helsing change Lucy from Undead to dead? He will do it by driving a stake through her heart and cutting off her head.
e) How will Van Helsing find Count Dracula? He will search for his hiding places.
f) What will Van Helsing do to kill Count Dracula? He will drive a stake into his heart and cut off his head.

Test

Page 124

1 a) 2 b) 1 c) 1 d) 1

國家圖書館出版品預行編目資料

吸血鬼德古拉 / Bram Stoker 原著 ; David A. Hill 改寫 ; 蘇祥慧 譯. —初版. —[臺北市] : 寂天文化, 2012.11　面 ; 公分.

中英對照

ISBN 978-986-318-050-0 (25K平裝附光碟片)

1.英語 2.讀本

805.18　101021301

原著 _ Bram Stoker
改寫 _ David A. Hill
譯者 _ 蘇祥慧
校對 _ 陳慧莉
封面設計 _ 蔡怡柔
主編 _ 黃鈺云
製程管理 _ 蔡智堯
出版者 _ 寂天文化事業股份有限公司
電話 _ +886-2-2365-9739
傳真 _ +886-2-2365-9835
網址 _ www.icosmos.com.tw
讀者服務 _ onlineservice@icosmos.com.tw
出版日期 _ 2012年11月 初版一刷（250101）
郵撥帳號 _ 1998620-0 寂天文化事業股份有限公司
訂購金額600（含）元以上郵資免費
訂購金額600元以下者，請外加郵資60元
若有破損，請寄回更換

〔限台灣銷售〕